A GOOD LIFE
CUT SHORT

JOHNNY GUNN

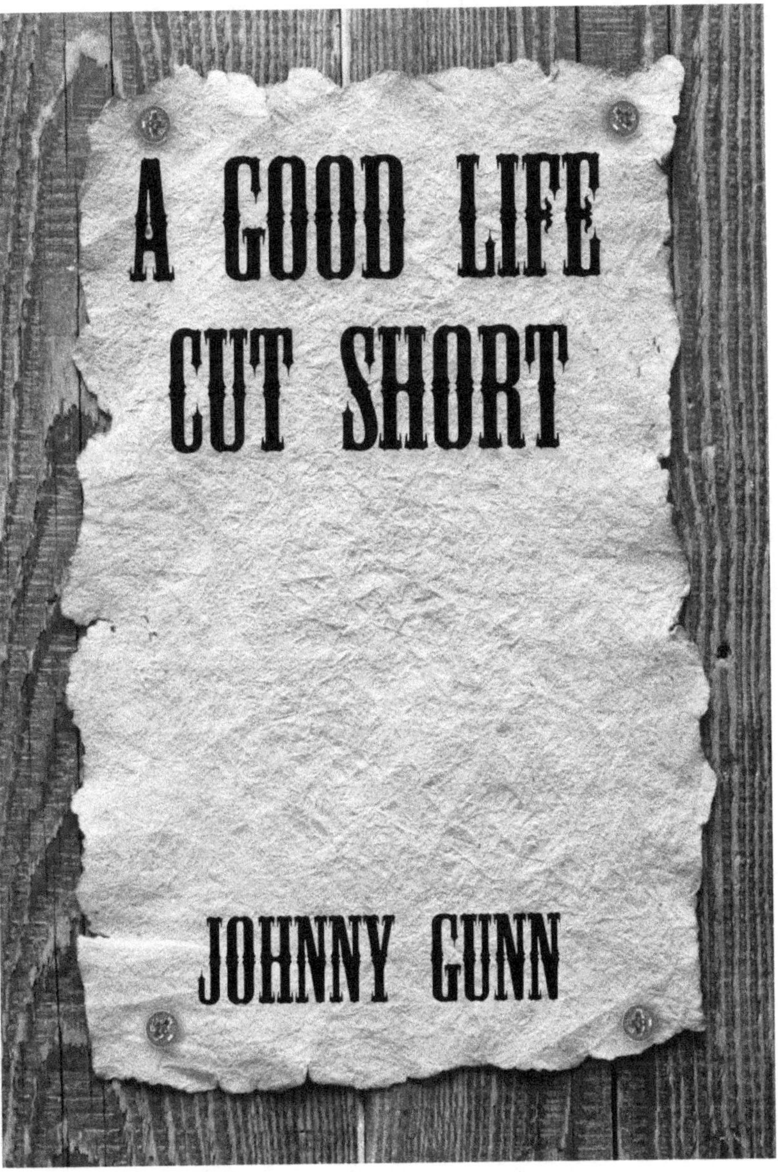

Cover Art:
Michelle Crocker

http://mlcdesigns4you.weebly.com/

Publisher's Note:

This is a work of fiction. All names, characters, places, and
events are the work of the author's imagination.

Any resemblance to real persons, places, or events is
coincidental.

Solstice Publishing - www.solsticepublishing.com

A Good Life Cut Short
A Jacob Chance, U.S. Marshal Novel
By Johnny Gunn

Dedication

This book is dedicated to the brave men and women of law enforcement who have fought the elements of crime to keep us safe.

Chapter One

"We're gonna miss you, Marshal," the young man in the U.S. Marshal's stables said, bringing Mr. Morgan out of his corral. Jacob Chance, U.S. Marshal, long and lean, his serape hanging loose and a slouch hat covering a full head of hair, took the reins of his Morgan stallion from the stable hand. His normally bright, inquisitive eyes had a touch of sadness to them.

"You take care of this fine piece of horse flesh. You really gonna get married?" The stable hand had started working at the San Francisco stables when he was just a boy, and every marshal in the district had great respect for the way he took care of all the animals.

"I've known you for many years, Freddie. Mr. Morgan and I are going to miss you as well. You've done a fine job taking care of this horse of mine. I want to take one of the pack mules, as well, if you could get one ready for me. I don't want to hurry you, but I want to catch that steamer for Sacramento, and it leaves in just two hours. Can we make it?"

It's been almost a year since Marshal Chance had promised Jennifer Stokes that he would resign from the Marshal Service, return to Golden Valley, Nevada Territory, and marry her. He spent that time closing cases, helping work on open cases, and wondering just what it would mean, to have a home to go to each night, to have a beautiful woman share his bed each night.

"And, yes, Freddie, I surely am going to get married."

Jacob Chance, now retired U.S. Marshal, knew he would make the steamer with no trouble, but also didn't want to get held up with a bunch of good-bye talk. It was hard enough just to actually walk into the Major's office and do it. The major wouldn't take his badge.

"No, Jacob, you might be retiring from active service, but I'm sure I don't have to remind you that the Service can and may call on you during times of great need. You keep that badge handy, my friend. We may find a use for a stove up old retired marshal down the road."

They laughed at that, knowing that one thing Jacob Chance wasn't, was stove up or old. "You make it a point, Major, to come to Preston and visit our ranch. My new bride is a beautiful young lady and her father is a fine citizen. He is one of the leaders of the community, and helped me set things straight on that job."

Chance couldn't help remembering what an ordeal it was in Preston, Nevada Territory, fighting a banker as criminal and dangerous as any he had met, and the banker's partner, a killer straight off the meanest streets in the world. His face hardened every time he thought about those days, gunfighters coming to town to kill him, a banker hiring people to kill and maim, and then that craggy, weathered face would soften, as he thought about Jennifer Stokes.

He left Major Randall's office with visions of Jennifer dancing through his mind. *What an amazing thing I've done,* he was thinking as he walked up to the stables. *I just quit the Marshal Service, I'm about to ride five hundred miles and marry the most wonderful person I've ever met. I'm about to find myself as a rancher, and Jennifer will be the first to tell anyone that I can't even throw a lasso.* He chuckled all the way across the plaza near the federal compound in the city and still wore a smile when he found Freddie bringing his horse out.

"It's a long ride to Preston?" Freddie asked.

"Yes, it is, Freddie. Over the massive Sierra Nevada, fighting spring thaw, then across the tall peaks of the White Mountains, and down into Golden Valley. It'll be a long ride, especially if I'm slowed because of thaw. I'm figuring a full two weeks on the trail, maybe longer if I run into raging rivers and lakes of mud."

Freddie chuckled, brushing Mr. Morgan to a black sheen. "You planning to take two weeks of supplies with you?"

"No, I'll resupply in Carson City or Bodie. The Carson route over the Sierra is filled with way stations now, and the road to Bodie is well used. The long haul will be Bodie to the Whites and over the top. It should be a beautiful trip this time of the year, with spring coming on."

He made up his packs and got them tied to the mule, started to step onto Mr. Morgan, when Major Randall hurried into the barn. "One last favor, Jacob," he puffed. "I have a prisoner that needs to be in Sacramento day after tomorrow. Since you're on your way, will you be official escort? It's Jaimie Boudrin, the man that tried to rob the bank in Sacramento and killed two people.

"He's still suffering some wounds and his court date for another robbery is in the capitol."

"If he's ready, bring him in. I don't want to miss that steamer. Better get another horse for out friend Boudrin, Freddie." Randall had the prisoner brought to the stables and Jacob found himself looking at a man with cuts about his face, including a split lip and black eye, one arm in a sling, and walking with a limp.

"Give me trouble, Boudrin, and you won't have to worry about prison," Chance snarled, mounting his horse and motioning the prisoner to mount up as well. He took the lead from the mule, shook hands with Freddie and rode onto the streets of San Francisco as a private citizen, but with a prisoner.

"Interesting way to retire," he muttered, "babysitting a killer." He had the lead rope for Boudrin's horse tied tight to the mule, and Boudrin's free hand was cuffed to the saddle horn.

How long has it been that I haven't carried a badge? From being named sheriff in that little mining town so many years ago to this. I've been involved in massive criminal cases, worked behind the scenes as a bad guy more than once, and have scars proving that a U.S. Marshal isn't invincible, and he caught himself snickering about that as he led the little parade down to the waterfront and onto a steamboat for the trip to Sacramento and the long journey to Golden Valley.

A horse handler took the animals and Chance led the prisoner to their stateroom where he cuffed Boudrin to a bedstead. Chance slipped out of his serape, re-pinned his marshal's badge on the buckskin shirt, and walked toward the doorway. "There were two men with you when you hit the bank, Boudrin, and you were the only one caught. If they might be looking to bust you free, they'll be just as dead as you," he said, stepping out on deck and locking the stateroom door. Boudrin had not said a single word since being brought to the stables.

Chance stood on the deck of the steamer and enjoyed the spectacle of the big side-wheeler moving away from the dock and into the bay. He felt the throb of the powerful engine as the ship began threading its way among hundreds of vessels, some steamers, some two and three mast sailing ships. It was a slow run out of the bay, through the delta formed by the confluence of the Sacramento River and San Joaquin River, then up the Sacramento River to the capitol city.

He asked that supper be served in his stateroom, rather than bringing the prisoner to the main dining area. "Are you anticipating trouble, Marshal?" the steward asked, taking the order for two suppers.

"Transporting a prisoner with a known reputation as a killer means I must anticipate every possible problem that might occur," Chance replied. "If there's trouble, I'm sure you would rather it happened away from your other passengers." The steward smiled and nodded, and Chance wondered if he really understood.

A gentle knock on the cabin door an hour later brought the retired marshal to full alert. *Too early for supper* flashed through his mind. He had his heavy forty-five revolver out and cocked when the door was splintered by a heavy boot and a huge man lunged toward him carrying a shotgun.

Chance's first round smashed through the man's chest and the second ripped his head into pieces. Chance dove to the floor, using the bed as protection when a second man thundered into the stateroom. Chance killed him with a single shot to his chest, stood and aimed the iron at Boudrin. "Any more coming?" he asked, placing the barrel of the gun against the man's nose.

"Non, non," the Frenchman screamed, trying to get away from certain death. Chance slammed the revolver across the man's head, knocking him unconscious, and walked out on the deck, letting those gathered know there was no more danger. The captain of the steamer and several sailors were on the scene immediately.

Both attackers were declared dead and their bodies were removed, and the captain had people in to clean up the stateroom. "I don't think we'll have anymore problem, Captain," Chance said, "but it will be best if we move to another cabin, if there is one."

A new cabin was found and Chance moved in and asked that supper be served right away. "A man gets hungry protecting prisoners," he quipped to Boudrin who cursed at him in several languages.

***

He arrived in Sacramento early the next morning and delivered his prisoner to state officials. "That horse belongs to the Marshal Service," he said. "Someone will be along to pick it up. Since his two companions made their move, I will forward my report to San Francisco so federal charges can be added to his problems. Regardless of what happens in state court, there is now another federal hold on the man," he said.

The spring air was filled with the aroma of fruit trees in full bloom as Chance made his way around the capitol. He purchased all the provisions he felt he would need for the ride over the Sierra Nevada Range and was well on his way to Placerville by late afternoon. It was the long steep climb out of Placerville and then the long steep drop to Lake Tahoe that would give him the most trouble, he was thinking, but for today, he said to Mr. Morgan, it would be a ride through the foothills to watch spring take over the California skies.

Along with a vast array of golden poppies, Chance enjoyed the sight of giant oak trees surrounded by lush grass, and often encountered orchards of fruit trees, in particular apple. Fields were being tended and there seemed to be a general bustling of activity along the road.

"How many thousands of men, mules, and wagons have been on this road since gold was discovered?" he asked Mr. Morgan, riding a well maintained highway into the foothills. Grass was green and the trees had blossomed a few weeks back. "Spring comes early in California," he mused, "and I'm heading into Nevada, where spring won't be arriving for a bit longer."

***

He wasn't making his fifty miles a day climbing through the granite trails across the Sierra, but he knew he would make it up when he got on the other side of the big range and started south. *I should come over a ridge not too far in front of me and look down on the emerald waters of Lake Tahoe pretty soon. I remember seeing that lake and the surrounding mountains the first time, back in fifty-seven I think it was. Before they discovered silver in Virginia City.*

That country I'm heading toward was called Utah Territory, and I remember that no one really was sure where the California state line was around that beautiful lake.

The wagon road, known as the Carson Road, seemed to be one way, in those days, with wagon after wagon heading west. What a poor sight it was. He remembered the empty look in so many eyes as the pioneers made their way over the Sierra Nevada. They had endured the plains, made it across the Rockies, then the more than formidable deserts of Utah Territory, and could almost smell California and the gold fields.

Now, those surrounding hillsides are denuded. All those trees ripped down and sent to the Comstock for the mines. I wonder if they'll grow back? He crossed the ridge and started the hard drop to the lake, enjoying the splendor of the lake's beauty and not appreciating the bare hillsides where once massive firs and pines grew.

He skirted Carson City and decided to make a run to Bodie for provisions before the long haul to and over the White Mountains. Bodie still carried the reputation of being a dangerous town, not as bad as Aurora, but close. He arrived mid-day, restocked as quickly as he could, and was on the trail to Mono Lake with plenty of daylight left.

Two days later, Jacob Chance found himself looking at the towering peaks of the White Mountains, knowing he was just a few days from Golden Valley and the start of a new life. "Tomorrow, boys, we'll start that long climb to the top of that pass right over there," he said to the horse and mule, "and we'll be camping in deep forest once again."

Camp that night was in a high meadow surrounded by huge pines and plentiful grass, with a spring-run creek gushing nearby. He hobbled the animals, found some dry wood and had a fire going in short order. *Looks like I'll be working through some snow and ice either tomorrow or the next day before we top off these mountains. They had a good winter and we'll have good water in Golden Valley.* His mind was filled with visions of Golden Valley, just over the highest ridge to his east. His coffee pot was boiling and he used the coffee to warm up some smoked venison he bought in Bodie.

"I've lived like this my entire life," he muttered, pouring a second cup. "Before the end of this week I'll be living in a house," and he had to snicker at that comment. "A house," he said again, aiming the words at his horse and mule. "You boys will be in stalls and fed out of a barn. Big changes coming our way, and this old retired marshal is half scared out of his mind."

***

It was on the third morning, after a steep climb through broken rocks and weather scarred trees that they topped off, and way in the distance, Chance could see Golden Valley. "Two more days, boys, maybe three, and we'll be home." He sat stock still in the saddle, realizing what he'd just said.

"Home," he said again, very quietly. "This is a concept that might take some getting used to," he laughed, nudging Mr. Morgan back into a strong walk. Chance's mind was filled with thoughts of Jennifer, the Golden Valley, a ranch and all the work that would go into running it, and being home each and every night. It was a pleasant three-day trip down from the lofty peaks of the White Mountains into the valley, and the long ride through the deep grass of the valley to the Stokes Ranch.

***

"There it is, Mr. Morgan, just as we left it last year, and look at how deep the grass is," Chance said, seeing the Stokes ranch about two miles up the trail. He rode into the main yard, not seeing any activity around the barns or corrals, and stepped off the big stud. He tied off the horse and mule and started for the veranda style porch when the main door was flung open and a hurricane came flying at him, a tornado in wild hair and billowing skirts, squalls of pleasure, and strong arms flung around his neck.

Chapter Two

The wedding was spectacular by any standard, but with Jerrod Stockton, that monster of a blacksmith director and producer, and Ben Stokes provider of beef, lamb, and pork, spectacular simply isn't strong enough of a word. It took three days with open pits filled with meat, every woman in the valley provided pies and cakes, and barrels of freshly brewed beer was poured, and the party was finally over.

Ben Stokes, Cotton Phelps, and Jerrod Stockton put together a crew and Jacob Chance discovered that he knew virtually nothing about how to build a house, a barn, or even a hog pen for that matter. "You've had a wasted life, Jacob," Jerrod teased him often, "just chasing bad guys never learning the good things, like carpentry, iron work, fence post digging."

The house was livable within a short amount of time and Chance carried Jennifer across the doorway into their new home. All the finish work still needed to be done, calves were being born daily, animals needed to be fed and watered, and as Jerrod pointed out, fence posts needed to be set. "A man could get tired living this life," Chance said one night as he and Jennifer called it a day.

"I have good news, Chance," she said, pouring them a cup of hot coffee. "We're gonna have a baby." He just sat there with a big dumb grin on his face as she cuddled up on his lap, running her fingers through his mop of hair, wrapping her arms around his head and squeezing hard.

***

For the next many months it was just hard work every day for both Jennifer and Jacob, and they discovered that Jennifer's brother James wasn't living up to what the judge had demanded of him. "James got his hundred and sixty acres, just like we did," she said one night, "and hasn't done a single thing on that property. He'll lose it, won't he?"

"Worse than that," Chance said. "Judge Stanfield was very strict with his demands of the man. He had to be productive, take care of his homestead, and stay out of trouble. That old judge is a tough man and James is liable to find himself heading to prison if he doesn't shape up." Chance could still recall the night young James Stokes attacked him in the hotel in Preston and how hard he and family had fought to keep the boy out of prison.

"He's being a fool, Jenny, but it's his choice."

***

Hard work on the ranch was paying off for Chance and Jennifer as their herd built up, and more and more outbuildings were built and filled with animals or equipment. Chance bought a beautiful Morgan stud and three mares from a friend in California's central valley, a Spaniard that bred Morgans. Along with cattle and sheep, Chance planned on breeding horses that would adapt to the high desert conditions in Nevada.

It was a long three week ride for the two of them, bringing the small horse herd in. They had the help of one Vaquero and procured a hand from Ben Stokes' crew.

The entire valley had one more party that year of 1864. On the last day of October, President Abraham Lincoln signed the official declaration naming Nevada the thirty-sixth state of the union. Of course that called for the roasting pits to be lit and for beef, lamb, and pork to be roasted, it called for anyone with a musical instrument to show up and play, and it called for every woman to dress in her finest and dance with every man that asked for the honor.

***

The first year seemed to "just whip by," Chance said the next spring, holding his young son, Little Jake in his arms, walking through a pasture with Jennifer as they counted calves. "How is it possible that we've been married a year, Jenny? It seems like a day or two ago that I rode into your father's ranch. Here we are, mama and papa Chance, with a beautiful baby and a building ranch."

"I've never met a man like you, Chance. If I didn't call you in, you'd work through the night, I think. Look at that house," she said, gazing off a quarter mile at their large two-story ranch house, surrounded with a covered porch, standing white in a field of deep green grass. "You did that, Chance. And just look at that little bundle you've got in your arms. You did that, too," she laughed.

***

The year 1864 became 1865, and before anyone was aware it was coming Christmas, 1866. Little Jake could almost walk, he sure was trying, Jacob's new Morgan stud had done his work with perfection and he had some very nice looking foals dancing in tall grass, and the cattle herd had grown significantly.

The only cloud on the horizon was young James Stokes. "I've given up trying or worrying," Jennifer said, one cold morning. "He'll lose that ranch, Chance, and it's a good one. Can we take it over?"

"I'd have to check on that, Jenny. I don't know. I'll send a letter to Judge Stanfield, maybe one to Major Randall. I'm going to be with your father most of the day, getting ready for our Christmas party. He's going all out, again. That man loves his roasting pits.

"You and Little Jake come over whenever you get ready. Buck Colby will help you with the buggy."

"I gave him the day off, Chance. He went into Preston to buy new duds for the party tonight. I think the whole valley is gonna be there. I can harness the buggy, and maybe I'll just wrap Jake in that blanket I made up and ride over instead of bringing the buggy. Little Jake loves to ride with me. 'Go Fast' he yells, and laughs loud when I let that horse run."

Chapter Three

"What am I gonna do about Jim? He didn't learn a thing from Judge Stanfield, Chance, not one damn thing. He's a snarly little kid in a grown man's body. Why are we gathering the wood? Why isn't he helping? If he wasn't my son, I'd throw him off the ranch."

"Maybe that's what you'll have to do, Ben. He needs to understand the reality of being an adult." Jacob Chance, is almost as upset with young Jim, as the old man. "I understand your reluctance, but he needs a good solid slap up the side of his head. That's what he needs."

Jim Stokes had attacked Chance when the marshal came to Preston, Nevada Territory in 1863, and the Stokes family along with Chance, worked with District Judge Amos Stanfield to get the boy on probation instead of sending him to prison. Stokes and Chance questioned whether they did the right thing.

"Looks like the weather's gonna hold, Chance." Ben Stokes was loading a wagon with split hardwood logs under a clear sky. The few clouds there were, billowed a bright white that almost hurt the eyes, and the breeze didn't carry icy threats of frostbite. "We get Christmas season weather like this, just once in a while."

"Certainly good timing," Chance said, hefting more wood onto the wagon. "How many times have you had an outside Christmas dinner, Ben?"

"One other time, back about ten years, maybe. Got away with that one, too," he laughed. "We'll have the one big pit for the side of beef, and then two smaller pits, one for the venison, and one for the fowl, goose and duck. We'll be feeding fifty people or more tomorrow night, if I can still count."

"I think you'd make a pact with the devil if it meant you could have your roasting pits fired up," Chance laughed.

"This is your third Christmas with us, Jacob. Seems like just yesterday when you rode into this beautiful valley. So many people in Golden Valley and in Preston still look on you as a savior."

"Nonsense, Ben. I was just doing my duty. That's what a U.S. Marshal does, clean up the mess made by those that can't be law-abiding citizens. That definitely was one big mess those fools made, though. I had a lot of help, if you remember. You, Jerrod Stockton, Hank Adams, Cotton Phelps, and I don't want to leave out Tiny Bidwell, all got behind me and we took out Colonel Dickson and Preston Miller, and their outlaw friends.

"No, Ben, I'm no savior, just a law dog doing his job. Not now, though," he laughed, tossing more wood in the wagon. "Jenny is working my skinny butt off trying to teach me how to be a cowboy. My roping is getting better, though, I gotta say, and our herd is building nicely."

"Do you miss the old work? You were in the Marshal Service a long time."

"There are times I think about being on the trail, but all I have to do is see Little Jake, put my arms around Jenny, look out across this valley of ours, and I know I did the right thing. That boy is growing so fast, and he's got such a warm personality, I would never go back."

Golden Valley is lush despite being in Western Nevada's Great Basin, generally described as desert. The Good Hope River bisects the valley, drawing its water from the towering mountains to the west. Some of the peaks of the White Mountains top eleven thousand feet, and provide excellent spring, summer, and early fall grazing for cattle raised in the valley.

"It's been two and a half years, Ben, and look what Jenny and I have put together. A nice herd of cattle, a building horse remuda, a large house, barns, and sheds, and best of all, a big, happy baby.

"No, sir, I could never give this up and return to the service. It would take a catastrophe to make me put that badge back on." They climbed up on the wagon seat and brought the wood to the home ranch, ready for the pits and tonight's big Christmas dinner.

"Do you even have any idea of how many people you might have invited to this shindig of yours, Ben?"

"Don't worry, Jacob, we won't run out of food or drink."

***

"I know I'm forgetting something," Jennifer Chance mumbled, as she moved around the large kitchen at her old home on the Stokes' ranch. "Yams, white potatoes, green beans, fresh bread, gravy," she was ticking off the pots and pans scattered around the large wood cook stove, and her mind wasn't really on today's Christmas feast.

It was two and a half years ago that Jacob Chance walked through that door, her mind reliving the moment. *Early spring, and that wonderful man won't ever leave. Is it even right for someone to be this happy?* Jacob Chance, U.S. Marshal had swept her off her feet at first sight.

"Now look at us," she mumbled, stirring the huge pot of gravy. "He built our home, we have a beautiful baby, and a growing herd of cattle and horses. It'll be three years in April, and this is our third Christmas."

"Talking to yourself?" her father asked, sticking his head close to a large pot of heavy, thick gravy.

"Just making sure, Dad," she said, shooing him away from the stove. "I guess I've got everything. Venison, beef, goose, and all those things are out there," and she pointed out the door, "where you should be. This will be the most wonderful Christmas I've ever had." She stopped, stock-still, that beautiful smile splashed across her face, and let her father take her in his arms.

"We've come a long way, Jenny, a long way." He gave her a peck on the forehead and started back out to check on all the meats roasting in open pits, surrounded by men. The guests from town should start arriving soon, but Chance and Stokes had put their ranch hands to work on the pits. All the ranch hands would be at the tables for dinner.

"We sure have," Jennifer muttered, letting her mind race back through the last couple of years. *Jacob retired from the Marshal Service, and that had to be the hardest thing he ever did. I know he misses that life, and I'm so glad he loves this new life.* She was almost in tears, tears of joy, is how she would describe them.

She let her mind continue to drift through their recent history as Mr. and Mrs. Jacob Chance. She and Chance, as she still called him, had spent hundreds of long, hard hours working to build their new home, build a herd of fine cattle, and learn everything they could about each other. There were few fights or arguments, mostly because they were too tired to engage in anything serious, and it really wasn't something either one enjoyed or wanted to do.

She remembered him learning to rope. "How can a man as old as you are not know how to throw a reata?" she whooped often while watching him. "Okay, you are standing still and the fence post hasn't moved a splinter," and she fell to her knees laughing when he missed.

Some men might get frustrated, maybe even a bit angry at that, but Chance just gritted his teeth and tried again and again. He had a little boy's grin across a well aged mug when he did find the fence post.

She could remember when he caught his first calf, horseback, and the Jacob Chance smile that lit up the entire Golden Valley. "Those calves are all gonna need brands and doctoring next week, oh mighty roper," she giggled, "so don't stop practicing."

Where he got her was in his horsemanship. He loved to train young, spirited horses, and he and Ben Stokes worked hours every week creating a remuda of cow horses that were the envy of the valley. "They want to learn, Jenny," he'd say, as she watched him teach a young horse to sidestep, or back up. "They need to have confidence in you, want to be with you, and it doesn't take long for them to grasp what it is you want them to do, and always, with you.

"Even though I'm not a cowboy, at least not yet," he grinned, "I know what the horses are supposed to do, so I can teach them. A horse is incredibly smart and they have good memories. That works if you're teaching them something, and it works the other way, too, if you are mean with them. You beat or whip on 'em, they'll find a way to get even."

She knew cattle, he knew horses, and the ranch was built around what each was very good at. He told her stories about working with a Mexican vaquero down in the Sacramento Valley of California. "That man would spend a couple of days just standing around in a corral with a young horse, and without saying a single word, would have the horse wanting to be with him all the time.

"I spent months working with that man and he taught me so much about horses, and in turn, people. That has helped me for all these years. Treat people right, most of the time they'll treat you right."

She found some good bulls in the Humboldt Basin of northern Nevada, and used them to build the herd. She was the trail boss and Chance and the other buckaroos respected that all the way.

She was smiling, remembering the first time Marshal Jacob Chance made a trail ride. *His horsemanship was excellent,* she remembered, *but his cow savvy didn't exist.* She was laughing out loud, stirring gravy and thinking about him trying to move heifers through heavy brush, getting them across streams and ditches, and not being very good with a lariat.

***

Ben Stokes was standing on the porch of the ranch house. "There's dust on the trail," he said, pointing it out to those standing around the big fire pits down below. "Wonder who our first guests will be today?" he mused.

"Jerrod should be coming with Eileen Sprague from the women's shop," Jacob said, mopping some good sauce on the large beef roast slowly being turned on a spit. "He fell as hard as an old oak when she moved to town."

"Maybe like someone else I know?" Ben joked. "Course this could be Sarah and Cotton, or even Hank Adams. Hank's back in Preston for a month from his duties in Carson City. Best thing we ever did was create that agency and let him represent the ranches and farms here in Golden Valley."

Chance watched the dust coming closer, remembering how many times he had made that ride from town to see Jennifer. "We're sure lucky on the weather, Ben. Couldn't ask for nicer weather at the end of December."

"I've been making my case for several weeks, Jacob, and I guess I was heard," Ben laughed. "Even when it's cold, if that sun's shining, it feels good. It's the wind that could spoil a day like today. As you said, we're lucky there's no wind." He had his head back, slouch hat in hand letting the sun pour down.

Three large fires were burning, each roasting some type of meat. The bunkhouse had been cleaned out and made into a large dining room. Along with many of the near-by ranchers, several people from Preston would be at this Christmas feast, and many of the buckaroos from the area's ranches would be in attendance as well. Several had been put to work helping with the cooking, cleaning, and serving.

Festive garlands of silks and other fabrics were hanging from the porches and some of the trees, lanterns were in profusion in the large open yard, and there were many who had discussed setting the tables up outside, the weather being that fair. "Jennifer already called it the best Christmas ever," Ben said, "and I sure am willing to agree with her."

There were flasks of fine wine and good whiskey on every table and in every man's hip pocket, and fruit punch for those not wanting to imbibe. As at every function, huge pots of boiling coffee were near every open fire.

Within minutes of Stokes spotting dust on the trail, Cotton Phelps drove his wagon into the ranch with Sarah and daughter Georgia sitting comfortably in the back. "Merry Christmas," Cotton hollered, bringing the team to a halt. He had the team unhitched and in a corral in a matter of minutes.

"Well, looks like we're not the first to arrive," Cotton said, shaking hands all around. "Sarah wanted to get here early enough to help Jennifer and Cookie in the kitchen. My heavens, that's a big chunk of steer there."

"Have a whole haunch of venison right over there," Chance said, pointing at another pit, where Jim Stokes was tending the spit, "And some big Canadian honkers roasting in those covered pans there. Jerrod shot them yesterday and dropped 'em off for us." He stood back from the hot fire and wiped his brow. "Anyone goes hungry around here today, it's their own fault.

"Don't let that flame flair up there too hot, Jim," he hollered over to young Stokes.

"I know what I'm doin'," he snarled, sprinkling some water on the flames.

"More dust," Ben said. "Bet this is Jerrod and Eileen."

***

Tension had been building for a couple of months between Chance and young Stokes, despite everything that Jennifer and her father could do. The man simply was not a working type person, rarely finished a job, did sloppy work when helping to build the new ranch house and barns, and refused to work with the animals.

"He doesn't understand that he's on probation," Jacob said so often. "Despite the lectures he got from Judge Stanfield, despite the fact the judge did not send him to prison for attacking me, despite the fact we helped him get his homestead, that fool does not believe that if he doesn't straighten up, he's going to prison. Stanfield asks about him in every letter we get, and I've been holding off telling the truth.

"Worse than that, Jenny," Chance said too often, "he's going to lose that homestead."

Jennifer spent hours trying to get her older brother to fall in line. Ben finally quit trying to talk to the boy, his temper flaring every time. "Ben still thinks all of Jim's problems are his fault," Chance told Jennifer often.

"He believes that he hasn't been a good father to the boy, but that simply isn't true." Chance spent more years dealing with criminals and ugly people than Jennifer had been alive, and he saw nothing but trouble in young Jim. "Your father gave him a loving home, warm clothing, good food, and taught him the things in life he would need.

"I won't go so far as to say Jim has an evil heart, but if he doesn't straighten out, he'll end up going to jail. Judge Stanfield was emphatic about that, if you remember. He's on probation and he doesn't care." Chance and Jennifer tried to work with Jim every chance they got, tried to involve him in projects that would benefit him and his homestead, and nothing seemed to work.

Planning for the Christmas dinner had included the entire family, but the only thing they could get Jim to do was slop mop-sauce on the venison haunch and keep the coals burning. He had been heard to say to some of the Stokes' hands that he might not even stick around for dinner.

"It's a bunch of crap," he said to Jacob one day. "Dad doesn't give a damn whether I'm at that dinner. All Jennifer does is yell at me, and you, ex-Marshal, treat me like a hired hand. I own most of this ranch," he stormed.

"No, you don't, Jim," Chance said. "Your father owns the main ranch, Jennifer and I own our homestead, and if you don't start working on yours, you'll lose it. The homestead law is pretty clear, and you're almost two years into a five year plan, haven't put up a building, haven't cleared pasture, don't even have a well or irrigation ditches. Jenny and I have promised you heifers and a bull to get your herd started, but you have no way to keep or build a herd."

"Go to hell," he said, and stalked off, leaving Jacob Chance to just shake his head. He told Jennifer about the encounter when they had supper that evening.

"He's been that way his entire life, Jacob. I doubt he'll ever take responsibility for himself or his property, ever."

"We spent a lot of time convincing that judge that Jim would straighten up if given a chance," Jacob said.

"The government is not going to give him the deed to that land, your father isn't going to let him slink back home, and I don't think we want him being an influence on Little Jake."

Jenny wanted to cry, tell him "no", but knew he was right. "Let's wait 'till the holidays are over, Chance, then maybe we can have a quiet talk with him, make him understand what it is he is losing."

***

"What an immense amount of food you have cooking," Sarah Phelps said, coming into the kitchen. "Where's baby Jake?"

"Hopefully he's taking a nap. Come on," and she walked out of the kitchen and down the hall to what had been her bedroom, growing up. Georgia was right with them, letting her long auburn hair flow in the breeze they created.

"You're twelve now, Georgia?" Jennifer asked, as they slipped into the baby's room. "Where does time go?"

"I'm almost thirteen. More than twelve-and-a-half," she said with the pride of an almost teenager. "Mama made me wear a dress for Christmas dinner. We made it last week. Just in time, huh?"

"Didn't dare make it any sooner," Sarah said. "She's growing an inch a week, I think. Oh, look. He's beautiful, Jennifer. Looks so much like you, but that chin and that hair, that's Jacob."

"Can he walk?" Georgia asked, reaching out and taking Little Jake's hand. "He's strong," she said, as he squeezed her finger. "You better get him a sister pretty soon, Jennifer. He's gonna need someone to play with."

"I'll work on that, Georgia," Jenny said, chuckling along with Sarah. "How about you change this little brat and keep him company for awhile. We haven't had this many people for supper in this old house for ages. It's way more than Cookie can keep up with." She gave Georgia a clean diaper and walked toward the door.

"Along with everyone Dad and Jacob invited, we have our regular hands also. That table will be groaning with food."

Chapter Four

Following the grand supper, during which every morsel was consumed, Jerrod Stockton led the group in singing Christmas carols. The huge blacksmith and his booming voice spread good cheer through the entire Golden Valley, Ben Stokes thought, sitting back in a large chair on the veranda. He watched the fires burn down to glowing embers, the stars sparkling in the winter night and enjoyed the warmth of a full belly.

Chance told Jennifer many times that without Jerrod, there would not be a Preston, Nevada today. "I came to this little village, run by gangsters, Jenny, and met this mountain of a man who backed every play I made. They beat him with ax handles, kicked his ribs in, and even tried to shoot him, I think.

"Now, they call him Mr. Mayor. Well, it's deserved. Every small town needs a Jerrod Stockton to act as the town's backbone. I pity the man who tries to cheat or rob that giant."

Several of the cowboys brought out more wood and got the fires blazing in the new cold air of Christmas Eve, many of them humming the carols that had been sung.

"I think they can hear you all the way in town, Jerrod," Stokes smiled, shaking his head "no" to the invitation to join in another sing-along. "Sit with me for a spell, Jerrod, and tell me what's the big news in Preston, now that you're the official mayor."

Stockton came up on the broad porch and found a chair to drag over by Ben, and settled his large frame down into its cushions. "It's been a long haul, Ben, but we are official now. With statehood, in Sixty Four, we became an actual part of Esmeralda County, and with all the help from

Judge Stanfield we have township status. The elections finalized everything.

"We have a town council, a justice of the peace, a sheriff, the whole mess," he laughed, waving off some of those by the fire that wanted him to lead some more songs. "I think we have done well, Ben." He sat back, looking up into the dark sky, and continued. "Jose Alvarado was elected sheriff and he is doing a really good job. Jacob has come to town a couple of times and given him some pointers. He worships that man, as so many of us do.

"Hell, Ben, we wouldn't even be here if it weren't for Jacob, and look at him out there, dancin' with Jenny, and he actually sang a couple of times." His booming laugh echoed about. "Whoee," he howled, "U.S. Marshal Jacob Chance performing tonight, ladies and gentlemen," and he slapped his knee, pointing at Chance, who laughed right along with him.

"Jenny has never been as happy as she has been these last two years," Ben said. "We're all worried sick about young Jim. He's reverting to the fool he was, and simply doesn't give a damn about anything."

"He's been in town several times recently, talking to Tiny Bidwell about running a faro table at the Crystal Saloon. Tiny doesn't want one, but Jim is always packin' that deck of cards. Well, you know how I feel about the kid," he said, and Ben remembered that Stockton wanted to shoot him the night some gunfighters tried to break Preston Miller out of jail.

"Chance is sure he's going to lose his homestead," Stokes said. "He hasn't done a lick of work on the place in two years. What a waste," he said, shaking his shaggy old head, as if defeated.

"You know as well as anyone, Ben, everyone has given him every opportunity to bring himself around. You're right, though, he doesn't give a damn." The two sat for a long time, watching the fire and those around it, some watching the stars gleaming in the night, others looking into bright eyes, sparkling with pleasure.

"Gettin' cold, Jerrod. Think I'll call it a night. Merry Christmas to you." They stood up and shook hands, and Ben slipped into the old ranch house. Jerrod returned to the warm fire.

***

"This is the most wonderful Christmas I've ever had, Jacob Chance. Did I tell you that Georgia thinks we should give Little Jake a sister? She says he needs someone to play with."

"Just what did you say to that?" he asked, a twinkle dancing in his eyes, and he patted her on the bottom, then pulled her in close to him.

"I said we would work on that," she said, just a bit of coy in her smile. He simply picked her up and carried her into the barn, slipping into one of the stalls filled with fresh straw.

"There's no time like the present," he said, and the two were engulfed in laughter, moans, and soft sighs.

"Where do you suppose those two are going?" Jerrod Stockton said to Eileen Sprague.

"You just hush, now, Mr. Stockton. They know what they're doing and it ain't any of our concern." She paused, letting her fingers massage a large turquoise stone, set in silver, pinned to her blouse. "Thank you for the brooch, Jerrod, it's very nice. I'm more and more glad I moved to Preston."

"I'm very glad you did," the big man said, turning several shades of scarlet, hard to see in the deep night. "Thank you for that knife. I've been a good blacksmith for a long time, Eileen, and I've never made a knife as fine as this one." He pulled it from a sheath on his belt and held it up to the light from the fires. "The best Christmas I can remember," he said. He wanted, so much, to put his arms around the lovely lady, and was terrified that she would not let him.

Eileen took the initiative and took one of his big, gnarly hands in hers, and held it close. "Merry Christmas, Mr. Stockton, Merry Christmas," and she pulled him down, giving him the finest gift he could think of.

"All right, you two, there're children around," Sarah Phelps laughed, walking near them. "Cotton tells me you two are going hunting in the morning?" she asked, patting the blacksmith on the shoulder.

"Yup. Couldn't get Jacob to come, but we'll have more roast goose and some ducks for the table this week. They're flying thick along the river.

"Hey, there you are, Cotton," he said as Cotton Phelps walked up to the fire and put his arms around Sarah. "Just talkin' about gettin' some birds tomorrow. How you feelin'?"

"Don't get me started, Jerrod. You knew that horse wasn't broke when you sold him to me, didn't you." Laughter rang through the crowd and Jerrod ducked a punch that was thrown half in jest. "Damn thing took me through two fences and dumped me in the pond for good measure.

"You need to know, Mr. Mayor, that horse now is one of my best stock horses, no thanks to your breaking technique. We moved three hundred steers into winter pasture, have at least four hundred fresh heifers to add to our herd, and that horse will get one fine work out every day."

Slowly, the party broke up, teams were hitched and hooked to wagons, horses were saddled and mounted, and the words "Merry Christmas" echoed through the tall cottonwoods around the Stokes' ranch house. Jenny and Jacob, mounted on good stock started off for the hour's ride to their homestead. Little Jake was wrapped in a blanket tied around Big Jacob's neck, sound asleep.

"Why didn't you want to go hunting with Jerrod and Cotton tomorrow, Jacob?" Jenny asked, as they rode side-by-side. "You'll never hear me argue about a possible roast goose supper."

"I would rather spend tomorrow alone with you and Little Jake. I was afraid this idea of not being a U.S. Marshal wouldn't work, Jenny, but I'm so happy, I just want to be alone with you guys. I've never had a home, spent many more nights under the stars than under a roof, lived pretty rough, and I like my new life. I just want to be alone with you and Little Jake."

If he had looked, he would have seen tears streaming across Jenny's face. "Me too," is what she whispered back. They had several conversations on the ride home, planning for their future, building a successful ranch, increasing the family, and worrying about Ben and young Jim.

Morning found fires lit and a big breakfast spread for the three. Chance came into the kitchen, covered in snow and ice. "Storm blew in just after we got home, I guess," he said shaking if off on the weather porch. "May be here for a day or two, I think. That wind is cold." She followed him into the living room, brushing more snow off his back.

"Where did you find this saddle?" Jennifer asked, pointing at a brand new saddle sitting on the floor. "It's beautiful." She cried when he brought it out for her after they got home and got Little Jake in bed.

"I had Hank Adams pick it up for me in Carson City. Good saddle maker up there, and he said the design is perfect for working cattle." He slipped his arms around her and pulled her close. "I was really worried that I wouldn't fit in, wouldn't be able to give up my roaming life, fighting all the time, never knowing if someone would pull a gun just because I wore a badge, but I want you to know, I've never felt more at home, more peaceful, more loved, than I do right now."

They were holding each other tight, rocking back and forth, enjoying the warmth from their love and the fireplace, when the battle cry of a hungry boy brought them back to reality. "No time for lovin' when Little Jake's hungry," Jennifer chuckled, breaking free from Chance.

"Oh, by the way," she said, "go look next to your rocker."

He gave her a peck on the forehead and walked across the floor to a big rocking chair that Ben Stokes had made for a wedding gift. A large package was sitting on the floor and Chance picked it with a smile a mile wide. "My reata," he whispered, tearing the paper loose.

"Oh, my," he said. "A braided Spanish reata. Where did you find this? Oh, my," was all he could say, over and over. "No calf will be safe when I learn to use this," he laughed, grabbing Jennifer who had returned, carrying the baby. "Merry Christmas."

Following breakfast she watched for several minutes while Chance loosened up the new reata, and started putting loop after loop over the closest fence post. "The Vaqueros in California use large loops, Jenny, and they don't put a lot of pressure on the calves when they're working them. It's beautiful to watch." He built a larger loop and promptly knocked his hat off. Even Little Jake joined in the laughter.

Chapter Five

Preston Sheriff Jose Alvarado was standing at the big red-hot potbelly stove, trying to ward off the cold from the storm that blew in overnight. He had a cup of boiling coffee in hand, and watched the town slowly come to life. He saw three riders come in from the south, hunched against the icy wind, their coats and blankets covered in snow. *Those boys have been on the trail for a while,* he thought as they passed by, pulling their mounts to a stop in front of Jerrod Stockton's livery stable. Alvarado noticed that each man wore his sidearm low, as a gunman would, and each carried a rifle in a saddle scabbard. *Those aren't hunters coming through,* he thought watching them dismount.

Something wrong, the words kept running through his mind as he sipped on the hot coffee. *I don't recognize one of them, and they are a long way from nowhere. No pack animals, no nothing but bedrolls tied to the saddles. In the middle of winter? That's just plain wrong.*

Roger Bullis, with his slight limp, came out of the livery office as the three stood waiting. Bullis moved to Preston about a year ago, from his home in Mississippi, still suffering from wounds he received fighting in the War Between the States. "Mornin' gents," he said. "Y'all lookin' to be with us for a spell?"

Bullis had a bright and open personality, told jokes and old southern stories with animation and humor, and the town took to him right away. When the elections were held, Stockton had put his name in the pot for Justice of the Peace, and the town elected him their first judge, overwhelmingly.

"You boys been ridin' for some time through this storm? Well, welcome to Preston."

"Ya, maybe so, we stay," a large man with long blonde hair, bright blue eyes, and a full, shaggy beard said in a guttural snarl. "You keep our horses. I am Gustaf, you are Stockton?" His remarks were short, crisp, and demanding.

"No, I'm Bullis. Jerrod is hunting this morning. He should be back later this afternoon. Is he expecting you?"

"Ya," Gustaf said. "I make beer, good beer, and he promised me land."

"As I said, he'll be back later today. The café is right down there," and he pointed it out, "the Crystal Saloon is over there, and I'll take care of your horses for you." He took the lead ropes from the three and led the horses through the barn and into stalls in the back. The three strangers headed across the snow covered and icy street to the Crystal Saloon. "Boys made a long ride, and they don't have a pack animal," Bullis muttered. "Damn fools, I'd say."

Gustaf and his companions, Jeremy Lawton and Sparks Thomas had made arrangements with Stockton to buy the property where Colonel Dickson's saloon and brewery had stood, with plans to open a brewery and saloon. The township had taken ownership of some of what Dickson said he owned, and some of what Preston Miller had said he owned before they were discovered to be the criminals they were, before Dickson died and Miller met his maker.

"Dickson always said that river water made the best beer in the west," Sparks Thomas said as the three walked into the Crystal.

"Shut up, fool," Lawton snarled. "Don't ever say that name again anywhere near this town. You're an idiot, Sparks."

"Ain't nobody heard me," Sparks snarled, walking up to the almost empty bar.

"Don't give that stuff that you heard him say anything. Ain't one of us ever met the man, ever talked to the man, ever even cleaned his damn boots. All we have heard are crazy stories that probably aren't even true, so shut your stupid mouth." Lawton was growling by the time he got through, and gave the impression he'd shoot the younger man for the least provocation.

There were two old codgers at the far end and a fat old man in a dirty apron behind the oak bar. "Gimme a whiskey," Sparks said, when Tiny Bidwell walked down to the three.

"Make it three," Lawton said, giving Sparks an ugly look.

"Been on the trail for some time, I'd say," Bidwell said, putting three glasses and a bottle up. "Welcome to Preston. Gonna be here long?"

"Bought some property from the city. Your mayor advertised in the Salt Lake News. Gustaf, here, is a fine brewer, and we hear this river has some perfect water for making beer. Any of the homesteads Stockton talked about still for sale?"

"There's probably a couple, at least. You'd have to talk to Jerrod about that." The three men took their drinks to one of the tables and Bidwell went down the bar to talk to the old guys at the end.

"That should get the story out right," Lawton said, sitting down. "What have you heard from that Stokes kid, Gustaf?"

"Stupid fool," Gustaf said. "Thinks he be one bad man. Keep him at a distance, Jeremy. He's just not very bright, brags about things he knows nothing about." He took a long drink of whiskey and poured another. "He said he worked for Dickson, and often saw the man along the banks of the river, sometimes with a shovel. That man in Denver said that Dickson buried a lot of gold along the river.

"Two people saying the same thing, and I believe the story." Gustaf's eyes seemed to light up every time the word gold came up, and in the three weeks the men had been on the trail from Denver, the word had come up often.

"Sparks, why don't you run across the street and get us some rooms," Gustaf demanded and dropped a couple of double eagles on the table for him. "Find out about hot baths, too," he said, shoving the gold coins to Thomas.

"I'm an errand boy, now," Sparks Thomas said, mostly to himself, as he picked up the coins and started out the door. "You better start treating me better, Gustaf," he muttered, making his way across the street to the hotel.

"As I started to say," Gustaf said, sitting back watching Sparks shuffle off. "Young Stokes is supposed to be in town sometime today. We gotta be real careful with him, Jeremy. He's damn near as fool-hearty as Sparks, and probably just as dangerous. I want to find that gold just as soon as possible, and then we can get out of here."

"I still think we're on a wild goose chase, Gustaf. Some guy you never heard of tells you about buried gold and you believed him? I'm along just for the fun of it, so don't let me get in your way."

"Gold, Jeremy. Gold," Gustaf said, those blue eyes burning with desire. "I want my pockets overflowing with gold coins."

"We'd be better off robbing a bank," Lawton said, pouring another glass of whiskey.

***

Alvarado waited until the young gunslinger left the hotel and sauntered up the street to the now rebuilt Hotel Preston. *We tore this old building to shreds, but it didn't take too long to rebuild it. Shame old Don Springer had to die. We should have named this in his honor,* Alvarado thought, as he strode up to the desk.

"Got names on our strangers?" he asked Marcia Whitman, the new hotel owner. "I guess we're still a little jumpy," he said with a smile. "That Dickson fool had so many outlaw friends, everybody that comes through town wearing their gun low is a suspect."

"I'm glad I wasn't here during those times, Sheriff. I like it nice and peaceful. Here you go, one man with just the name Gustaf, one named Jeremy Lawton, and that wise-guy kid is called Sparky Thomas.

"Names mean anything to you? I've never heard of 'em," Marcia said.

"Jerrod told me about this man, Gustaf. He's been running a brewery near Denver and wants to buy the old Dickson saloon site to start a brewery here."

"Seems strange, doesn't it? Sell a lot more beer in Denver than here," Mrs. Whitman said, shaking her head. "Anyway, Merry Christmas Sheriff, and give your pretty wife the same from me."

"Feliz Navidad to you, Mrs. Whitman, and I sure will." He pondered what she said about selling more beer in Denver than Preston as he made his way down the street toward Stockton's livery. *The town is building, but she's right. Why come to Preston to build a brewery? Carson City? Virginia City? Not Preston.*

He saddled his horse for the long ride to the Chance Ranch and a talk with the former U.S. Marshal. As he rode north along the banks of the Good Hope River he watched clouds boiling over the White Mountains to his west.

We are in for another big storm of the winter, he thought, feeling the cold air through his heavy Mackinaw jacket. *That was a good storm last night, but this one looks even bigger. I've been cutting and splitting wood since September. I hope I have enough.* He was smiling, knowing he had at least seven cords ready for the next few months. *This snow and wind from last night is just a warning.*

He felt the snow blast through the wool of his Mackinaw, driven by gale force winds and had to laugh when he saw two ducks fly low and fast, landing on the Good Hope River. *Cotton and Jerrod are somewhere out there, and they think they're having fun.* He just shook his head, still wondering about the three strangers.

***

Jim Stokes left the Christmas party well before the food was served and rode into Preston. He kept a room at the hotel and spent several hours at the Crystal Saloon, but unable to entice anyone into a card game. Bidwell didn't keep a gambler on the books but did allow people to do what they wanted as long as they didn't create trouble.

"People are scared of me," Stokes said, shuffling and playing with the cards, standing at the bar.

"You talk mighty big, Jim, but I can tell you for sure, ain't no man in Preston afraid of you." Bidwell wiped the bar down, chuckling to himself. "They don't want to play cards with you because they don't trust you. More than one man has come close to calling you out, boy."

"You got no call to talk to me like that," Stokes snarled. "I ain't never cheated nobody and you know it. If you're calling me a cheat, I'm gonna call you out, old man." That Stokes' anger flared immediately, stirred some by bad whiskey, nursed by a lack of common sense.

"Just telling you what I see and hear, boy. Get yourself under control, finish your drink and skidaddle. Ain't no one wants to play cards with you and I don't want your business tonight. You're a trouble maker, Stokes, and I don't like trouble makers in my bar."

Stokes slammed his drink glass on the bar, spilling a bit, stared long and hard at the barkeep, itching to pull his iron and shoot the fat old man. Finally, he drank the whiskey and stalked out the door. "Go to hell, Bidwell," were his closing remarks, said as much to the great outdoors as to Tiny.

"That boy's gonna end up in lots of trouble," Bidwell grumbled, walking down the bar to talk to a couple of regulars. "One of you boys ever played cards with Stokes?" They both shook their heads no, and the conversation ended.

***

"Morning, Jacob," Sheriff Alvarado said, stepping from his big bay stallion. "How's your breeding program going? You'd make a good Vaquero, my friend."

"Good morning to you, mi amigo, and Merry Christmas. I love how the Spanish breed and train their horses, Jose, as you well know. You were raised on a Spanish ranch in California, so you know, too, how they work. I'll have Golden Valley bred, raised, and trained horses for sale come spring.

"What brings you way out here on a cold Christmas morning? Sheriff work?"

"'Fraid so, Jacob. Three strangers came to town this morning. Hope to hell you don't know any of them," he smiled. "Jerrod has been selling some of the property around Preston that Dickson and Miller owned, and using that money as, what he calls, seed money for the town treasury."

"Judge Stanfield gave him the okay for that," Chance said. "Seems like a pretty fair way to dispose of the property, make some money for the town, and get some new businesses open.

"Let's go in the house where the fires burn and the coffee's hot. Standing out in the middle of a blizzard is what Jerrod and Cotton would do, not two fine law dogs," he laughed, getting the door open.

"That was the idea," Alvarado agreed. "That's prime property where Dickson's saloon sat. Large enough for many uses. Anyway, one of the men coming in this morning goes by the one name, Gustaf. He supposedly bought the old Holiday saloon site and is planning a brewery there. Seems, though, that he owned a brewery in or near Denver. Along with him is a fella that looks a lot like a gunslinger. Goes by the name of Jeremy Lawton. Short, stocky as hell, and wears a full-blown mustache that droops below his chin.

"The third is a cocky kid named Sparks Thomas. He carries a swagger you can see for a mile. Any of those names ring a bell?"

"Jerrod mentioned this Gustaf guy, but I don't recognize the others, at least by name. Not much help I'm afraid, Jose. Something comes up, let me know, and don't forget the big horse sale come spring," he laughed, poking at the sheriff.

They talked horses and weather for half an hour, hearing the wind whistle about the big house, worrying about three visitors to Preston. "Guess I better get back while I can still see the trail," Alvarado said, slouching his way into his now warm Mackinaw.

"I'd be mighty proud knowing I was riding a Jacob Chance bred ranch horse, Jacob. Mighty proud," and the two shook hands. Jacob stood at the corral fence watching Jose Alvarado begin the long ride back to Preston, braving the now raging storm.

Town's good luck having that man as sheriff, he was thinking, scratching at his beard, letting one of his two year old colts mess with his sombrero. He settled his serape in place, rubbed one of the horse's ears, and walked toward the ranch house. *I could use a cup of coffee and a little conversation with a pretty lady.* He was wearing a smile as he walked into the kitchen, watching Jennifer feed Little Jake some lunch.

"I was watching you on that little gelding, Jacob Chance," Jenny said, giving her husband a big smile. "You really have the touch. You can't throw a lariat for nothin'," she smirked, "but you sure can teach a horse what the world is all about."

"Humph," is all he said, as he walked to the stove and poured a cup of boiling coffee. "That boy does eat well, Jenny. He's gonna be a big one." He sat down, tickled Little Jake, pinched Jennifer, and sloughed some coffee into a saucer, blowing on it, gently, before sipping some.

"You got something on your mind?" she asked.

He sat still for a moment, blowing lightly on the coffee, looking deep into her eyes. "I could get fat and soft being a rancher," he said, very softly. "Did I do the right thing, Jenny? Am I doing the right thing? We have three men working for us, and I'm not doing very much work."

"Now, you just hold it up right there, Mister ex-U.S. Marshal Jacob Chance. You have created a herd of finely bred and trained ranch horses, we have several hundred very pregnant heifers out there eatin' grass you planted and irrigated, we have fenced corrals and holding pens that you built, and we have a fine house that we built.

"You sound just like my father," she said, scowling through a hidden smile. "He'd work twelve hours and complain because he didn't get everything done in one day. Now, you just sit there and give me a little boy smile, let me tousle your hair just a bit, and if we're lucky, Little Jake will take a nap and we'll be very alone for more than an hour."

"The day I met you, Jennifer Stokes, Mrs. Chance, I knew I would be a happy man," he said, helping her tuck their boy into his bed, and ushering her down the hallway toward their bedroom. "A very happy man."

***

It was later in the day when the conversation with Sheriff Alvarado came back to him. He was in the barn raking some straw about, trying to make sense out of the conversation. He walked up to one of the stalls where a very pregnant mare stood at the gate. "Why would a man with a successful brewery in Denver want to move to Preston?" he asked her, rubbing one of her ears. "There has to be a reason other than good water makes good beer.

"Who's he gonna sell it to?" He grabbed the rake and moved some more straw, working the question back and forth. "I wish I had a way to know about those three men. I think I'll send a letter to Major Randall, see if there is any background on this man called Gustaf." He couldn't get the thoughts out of his head for hours, and was planning to take the letter to Preston first thing in the morning.

He headed back to the house when he saw two riders approaching through the storm. "Morning Jacob," Jerrod Stockton hollered, as they got closer. "See you two survived that feast we had last night." He held a large Canada goose and two Mallard ducks in his hand. "Old Cotton and I had a good shoot this morning, so we thought we would talk you out of a couple of pots of coffee to warm our frozen bones in trade for some meat for the table."

"Come on in, you two. There's always a pot of coffee boiling away. Besides, I want to talk to you about something."

They tied off their horses and shook as much snow as possible from their heavy coats, following Jacob into the warm kitchen. "Got company, Jenny, and dinner for later," he said, ushering the two men in. "Look at the size of that goose, Jennifer. Enough for four people."

"What did you want to talk about, Jacob? Something happen last night after we left?"

"No, nothing like that. Alvarado came out to visit this morning with news of three men that rode into Preston this morning. One is named Gustaf and he said he bought the old Dickson property. Something just sounded strange about all of it."

"Yeah he said he was coming. He owned a brewery in Denver, wanted to build one in Preston, and I told him about Dickson's brewery and the good water in the river."

"Didn't it seem strange to you that if he had a brewery in Denver he would give that up to build one in Preston?"

"Sure did, Jacob, but he sounded so sincere, and after all, I am the mayor, looking to put money in the city coffers, I couldn't very well tell him no."

"According to Alvarado, this Gustaf feller showed up with a couple of men that looked more like gunslingers than brew masters. You better keep your eyes open. What do you think, Cotton?"

"Sounded strange to me the first time I heard the story," Phelps said, pouring second cups for he and Stockton.

During his conversation earlier, Alvarado didn't mention that the three arrived in town with no pack animals and no material other than bedrolls tied behind the saddles. Preston, Nevada is at least two hundred miles south of Carson City, and the nearest community, Bodie, is on the other side of a major mountain range.

The big blacksmith shook his head, but with a smile on his face, said, "It is strange, I agree, but the man said he had cash money for the property, and if he wants to build a brewery to take care of our little valley, then I'm all in favor." He looked over at Jennifer. "Did this big galoot give you that saddle or did he keep it for himself?"

That broke the tension, and another pot of coffee was put on to boil. "It's beautiful, Jerrod. As soon as this storm breaks, I'll have it on a horse and we'll get it broke in right."

"Have you had a talk with Hank Adams?" Stockton asked Chance. "He's got some plans cooking about a feed lot in Carson City."

"He was here a couple of days ago and we spent several hours going over his ideas, all of which, by the way, are solid ideas. The northern half of the state is well populated compared to where we are down here, and we do have a difficult time getting a market for our cattle, despite the fact they are excellent."

"It's a long drive from here to Carson City," Cotton Phelps said. "Hank wants all of us to join our herds for a single drive to stock yards that he is planning in the north. If he gets it all done, it will be the best thing for all of us down here." As with Jennifer, Phelps had been around the cattle business for many years.

"I talked about Hank's ideas with Ben and with old Ed Kiefer, and a couple of others, and I think it's solid," Cotton said, getting a nod from Jennifer.

Chance looked around, getting nods from everyone, and said, finally, "I guess that seals it, then. Let's get all of us together with Hank, sometime soon, and get the plan finalized and all of us signed on."

"It would be one hell of a drive north," Cotton Phelps said. "Your herd, mine, Ben's, and two or three smaller outfits, and we're talking one big drive. Sure wouldn't want to take them over the White Mountains before heading north."

"No, we'd want to follow that long valley on the east side of those mountains over there," he said, pointing at some rocky hills that outlined the east side of Golden Valley. "That valley splits, and if we took the herd to the left fork, it would take us right around Walker Lake and toward the Carson River."

"Glad you know this country," Stockton said.

"We should ride that, Chance," Phelps said, "before Hank gets things all put together. We could have that trail laid out in our heads, know where we might have problems, know where all the water is. We would also know how many hands we might need to make the drive."

"I want to be with you," Jennifer said, quickly and seriously. "You're a fine cattleman, Cotton Phelps, and so am I. Chance, you know the country, but not from the point of view of a cattleman. I want to ride with you."

"Signed, sealed, and delivered, Jennifer. I would want you to," Chance smiled. "Let's set those plans for right after we move the cattle to high ground come spring."

Cotton Phelps and Jerrod Stockton bundled up against the blowing, howling blizzard for their rides. Cotton had a long ride to his ranch and Jerrod's was longer, all the way back to Preston. "At least we'll eat well," Stockton hollered, riding out, several geese hanging from his saddle horn.

Chapter Six

"That old fool, Gustaf, doesn't want us seen together, Big Jim, but I think you and me are so much smarter than that German Baron, or whatever he thinks he is. We could have our own gang, you know that? To hell with Jeremy and Gustaf, we'll form our own gang and have all kinds of good times." Sparks Thomas, twenty-three-years-old was itching to cause trouble anywhere, anytime, and young Jim Stokes, about the same age, was ready to ride with him.

Unknown to either Chance or Ben Stokes, Jim Stokes had maintained contact with some of Colonel Dickson's former employees, one of whom was living in Denver. Known as a card shark and burglar, Tyrus Watson, originally from St. Louis, was enjoying himself by spreading rumors that Dickson had buried thousands of gold coins along the Good Hope River.

His maps, vague in every respect, were not exactly selling like oysters and champagne, but they kept him in beer. He struck gold when he was introduced to Gustaf and the two worked well together. Gustaf paid Watson three dollars in gold for his map of the Good Hope River and possible burial sites allegedly filled with gold.

Watson helped Gustaf with a burglary of one of the saloons in Denver and had passed Stokes's name off to him as being a former Dickson employee, and one who could be a big help in locating all the wonderful gold. Stokes wasn't bright enough to understand Watson's joke and immediately offered to help Gustaf when the German brew master contacted him.

Neither Stokes nor Sparks Thomas had ever completed a job, fulfilled an obligation, or taken responsibility for their actions, and were willing to break any law, edict, or rule if it suited them at the time. They were ripe for the outlaw lifestyle, and too stupid to understand its consequences. A great man once said, 'an ignorant man can learn, a stupid man won't.' Sparks and Stokes would prove the axiom.

"I'm so tired of people telling me what to do, when to do it, how to do it, and knowin' that I'm smarter than they are, just makes me angry," Stokes said, rolling a smoke, sitting at a table in Tiny Bidwell's Crystal Saloon. He and Sparks had been told not to join Gustaf and Lawton in whatever those two had planned for the morning. The fire of anger was built on a kindling base of rotgut whiskey.

Stokes was still angry from Bidwell's ejecting him from the saloon the night before, and he seethed with rage. "Bring us another bottle," Stokes yelled, "and be quick about it."

"You ain't paid for the last one, Jim," Tiny said from behind the bar. "Credit don't work in this business."

"My father's good for it, old man. Just bring the bottle." The anger swelled as he slammed his fist onto the table. "Don't need no lecture from a wrung out barkeep."

"Nobody has credit here, Stokes. Pay up or get out." Bidwell fumed that the young man would expect his father to pay for his drunkenness. "Put that ranch together and make some honest money, and you can drink here anytime you want, but not until."

"Why you sniveling old man," Stokes howled, jumping to his feet and pulling iron. "I'll teach you to talk to me that way," and he pulled the trigger, once, twice, three times, before grabbing a bottle off the bar and urging Sparks Thomas to run with him to their horses. The two high-tailed it south, laughing, shooting through buildings on the way out of town.

"Looks like the Stokes' Gang has just been formed," he hollered at Sparks as they crossed the river a couple of miles south of Preston, and struck out cross-country. "Let's turn north and find us a nice full bank to fill our pockets, Sparks," he laughed, riding his horse through thick brush and heavy snow at a full gallop, snow, dirt, and rocks flying through the air along with the foul language from the two men.

The winter storm had howled for two full days with below zero temperatures, wind screaming through the valley, and snow measured in feet, not inches. A prudent man would not ride out into a blizzard at breakneck speed with no supplies. Being half drunk was not an advantage.

***

Sheriff Alvarado ran down the main street of Preston at the sound of gunshots, watched Stokes and Thomas ride out fast, and found Tiny Bidwell bleeding heavily from a gunshot wound to his upper chest, on the right side. "Find Stockton and get him here fast," Alvarado yelled at a forming crowd. "Who did this, Tiny? Who shot you?"

"That fool Jim Stokes," Tiny gasped, pain searing through his body. "He shot three times," he said, moaning from the pain. "Him and that jackass Sparks Thomas, but it was Stokes that shot me."

The sheriff eased Bidwell's head down, trying to stop the bleeding when Jerrod Stockton raced into the saloon. "My God," is all he said, grabbing a handful of bar rags and kneeling next to Bidwell. "Take it easy, Tiny, I'll take care of you. Looks like that bullet missed your heart and your lungs, but I gotta stop that bleeding."

Alvarado jumped to his feet and ran outside, nodding to two men to join him. "Pete, I need you to get to the Stokes' ranch as soon as possible and tell Ben what's happened here. Randy, will you ride with me? We need to catch that little bastard and whip his ass."

Randy Beuller still had his shopkeeper apron on, and said yes. "I'll grab my rifle, saddle up and meet you in front of the jail as fast as I can get there, Jose. Stokes has tried to be a bad man for years. Looks like the young fool made it this time. This will kill old Ben," he said, racing back to his store.

The two men were on their way out of town within ten minutes, found where Stokes and Thomas left the trail and crossed the Good Hope River. "Looks like they're trying to swing north, Randy. Not too hard picking up their trail through this country. Not snowing hard enough to hide their trail. Let's not kill the horses," he said. "We'll just follow the trail. They are riding awfully hard, so we'll just be steady with ours. At the rate they're riding, their horses will give out and we should catch them within a few hours."

Both men had taken the time to tie bedrolls to the back of their saddles and were wearing heavy Mackinaw jackets. "I grabbed a chunk of beef that might cook up pretty nice tonight, if we don't catch those little fools by nightfall," Randy Beuller said. "It's gonna be another cold one tonight."

The trail north that Stokes and Thomas were making took them out of Golden Valley, across a ridge of high rocky hills, and down into a long valley if they stayed their course. "Looks like they're gonna skirt Silver Peak well north, Randy. I wonder if either one has any concept where they're heading?" The sheriff and Beuller followed them into the rocky hills, noticing that the two outlaws were still pushing their animals very hard.

"Those horses will quit on them, Jose. You've seen that before," Randy said. A horse in good condition could recover fast if allowed to, but would simply quit when it reached a certain point. Alvarado and Beuller moved higher into the rocks, slowing their horses even more. The snow on the ground gave way to dirt and rock; the higher they climbed, mostly due to strong bitterly cold winds. "There's a trace of dust up there a mile or so," Randy pointed out as they moved onto a plateau that stretched a couple of miles before dropping into a long valley running almost due north.

"Let's go as slow and quiet as we can," the sheriff said, watching the tendrils of dust blow in the gale. "If they know we're behind them, they'll hole up and try an ambush. If we're lucky, their horses will just quit on them." They rode single file at a walk for about half an hour, seeing the dust swirls every few minutes.

"They've slowed their horses, Sheriff," Beuller said, pointing out the change in prints on the trail. "Can't ride a horse as hard as they've been doing and expect him to just keep going. They've slowed way down."

The trail through dusted snow and large rocks stood out as if painted on the landscape and every change in pace or direction was easily read. "They don't give a damn whether they're being followed," Alvarado said. "Keep an eye out, because if those horses give out, those boys will take to the rocks and we'll be the target."

The trail kept climbing, and the closer to the top of the ridge they rode, the rocks got larger, giving the outlaws and the lawmen cover if they needed it. "That's where they'll be," Alvarado said, pointing. "Looks like they're stopping, Randy. Let's tie off and move up on 'em nice and slow. Bring your rifle." They tied their horses to some Piñon trees and moved slowly through the rocks toward where they thought the two thugs might be. They could hear loud voices as they closed in.

Stokes was screaming angry when his horse simply refused to take another step, and he was ready to whip the animal when Thomas shushed him. "Quiet, Jim. There're people coming behind us." The two dashed around some rocks, found a likely place for an ambush and waited. It was just minutes when Stokes saw Randy Beuller slip behind a rock not fifty yards from him. He raised the rifle, waited, Beuller made a move for the next rock and Stokes shot him.

"Come on, we gotta get out of here," Thomas said. They ran back to their horses, barely cooled down some, mounted, and moved out at a bare trot. Two shots were fired, but nothing was hit as they moved down the side of the mountain toward that long valley. "We can't ride 'em hard, Jim. Gotta let them get their wind or we'll kill 'em for sure."

For one of the few times in his young life, Jim Stokes actually listened to some good advice. "We'll find water and set up for an ambush," Stokes said, as if the whole thing of taking care of the animals was his idea.

"We can make Ione by tomorrow, Jim. There's a big mine nearby. I know there's a bank and probably a big saloon. We can rob both. The Sparks and Stokes gang will be talked about all over the west," he laughed, as the two rode down the north slope of those mountains and into that long valley.

"How come you know about that?" Stokes asked. "I ain't never been out of Golden Valley since we moved there a long time ago. What kind of town is Ione?"

"It's the county seat for Nye County and we came through there coming to Preston. Ain't much of a town, though. There were lots of Indians, lots of miners, and lots of gold coins on the bar when we were there. The bank was right across the street, I think. Jeremy said it looked like easy pickins."

"Damn me, Sparks, this is just what I've been waiting for all my life. I was ready to ride for Colonel Dickson until that marshal showed up. He married my sister and that gave him the right to tell me what to do? He did not have the right to order Jim Stokes around. No sir, he didn't have that right.

"We'll show them what real outlaws are. Banks full of gold are lined up and ready for us to clean 'em out, Sparks. Ain't no one ever gonna tell me what to do, ever. Let's ride to Ione."

***

"How bad is it, Jose?" Randy Beuller asked as the pain cascaded through his leg. He could see blood soaked through his pants leg.

"Looks like the bullet broke your leg, Randy. I'll get the blood stopped, put a splint on, and get you back to town."

"No," the shopkeeper said. "No, go get those bastards. I'll be okay."

"Doesn't work that way, Randy. We'll get 'em, just not today." He fashioned a bandage and wrapped it around the wound, cut some limbs from one of the pines and made a splint, then helped the large man onto his horse. "This is gonna hurt, Randy," he said, boosting the shopkeeper into the saddle. "Bein' as cold as it is might be a good thing, and it will keep that wound from bleedin' heavy.

"Gonna be a tough ride back, so we can stop anywhere along the trail when the pain gets too much for you."

"I wish you'd just go get 'em, Jose. I can take care of myself." The sheriff didn't bother to answer, just moved on down the trail they had made, back toward Preston. It was a few stops and several hours later that they arrived in town, Beuller almost unconscious from loss of blood and the continual pain from riding. Pete Morrison, Ben Stokes and Jacob Chance were waiting for them at the jail.

"Better get big Jerrod Stockton down here," Sheriff Alvarado said as they pulled their horses up at the hitching rail. "Randy took one in his leg. Those fool boys are heading north, probably toward Ione, or maybe farther north toward the Humboldt country." He got off his horse as Ben Stokes and Jacob Chance helped Randy Beuller off his, Beuller grimacing with pain.

"I think the splint hurts as much as the damn bullet," he said as the men helped him to a chair in the jail office. "Don't let Maggie see me like this. Wait until Jerrod gets me patched up a little bit," he said as Morrison sprinted up the street to find the blacksmith/mayor.

"How's Tiny?" Alvarado asked, taking a cup of coffee offered by Stokes.

"He'll live, according to Jerrod," Jacob Chance answered. "Bullet went clean through him. Bidwell's more angry about Jim breaking all the bottles behind the bar with his stray shots," he chuckled. "That boy just crossed the line, Ben. We can't save him this time."

"We did everything we could, Jacob. Everything," the old man said, anger boiling as hot as the coffee in the tin cup he was holding, and all that anger was coupled with sadness, knowing he'd just lost his only son. "We were wrong in protecting him and keeping him out of jail for attacking you.

"I guess I've been doing that all my life. Protecting him, letting him get away with being surly, not finishing any job he ever started. I'm afraid I'm as much to blame for the way he is as he is."

"No, Ben. This isn't your fault. If it was, then Jenny would be much like Jim, and we both know that's not the case. Don't blame yourself."

Chance paced around the office for a few minutes, rubbing his chin, staring at the walls, the floor, finally settling into an old cane chair near the wood stove. "I'll ride out in the morning, notify the judge, and you know he'll demand immediate arrest. Maybe when Jim sobers up he'll realize what he's done and come back, but I doubt it."

"You want somebody to ride with you, Chance?" Sheriff Alvarado asked.

"No, I ride fast and long on a job like this. I'm going back to the ranch now, make sure Jenny and Little Jake will be okay and head out before first light. I know you're worried Ben, but Jim brought this on all by himself, and he'll have to pay the consequences. Keep an eye on my family, Ben."

"I will, Jacob. I know what you're saying about Jim, but he's still my son," and the old man was almost in tears thinking of all the things that could happen over the next days, weeks, or months. "How could I have a daughter who turned out as fine as Jennifer and a son who turned out to be such a rotten apple?" No one tried to answer and the gloom was broken with the arrival of Jerrod Stockton.

"Spending more time patching up the citizens than I do being their mayor," he laughed coming into the office, shaking off the cold of a bitter late December night. "Let's see what we can do about this little mess you've got in, Randy," he smiled, untying the splint and peeling the bandage off the wound. "Morrison went over to your place to tell Maggie what happened, make sure she knows you're gonna be fine." Stockton had spent so much time over the years doctoring and caring for large animals, that he was very calm and gentle treating all types of injuries. He loved to tell people, "You gotta remember, most of my patients kick and bite when you accidentally hurt them."

He helped Randy into the back of the jail where he could get him laid out on one of the cell beds, pulled up a chair, and started to work. "Ain't never been in jail before," Randy quipped. "Don't even think about closing that big ol' iron door."

Chance took that time to slip out the door and start the long ride back to his ranch. "Looks like we're back on the trail of a bad guy, Mr. Morgan," he said to his horse as they rode out of town. "Some people just can't be helped," he mumbled, remembering how he and Jenny and Ben had tried so hard to get Jim Stokes to ride the straight trail.

It turned out to be a beautiful night, the wind easing off, clouds breaking up, and a sky lit with millions of glittering stars. "I wish I could enjoy what I'm looking at," Chance commented, nudging Mr. Morgan into a long trot, both of them blowing great billows of steam from their mouths and noses.

The temperature was well below zero as he rode along the banks of Good Hope River toward home. "I like that thought," he muttered. "I'm going home. Haven't been able to say that since I was a little boy. Damn you, Jim Stokes." He could feel the top layer of snow slowly turn to ice as he slowed down from a trot to a walk. "No, sir, Mr. Morgan, I'm not gonna ruin your legs and feet crunching through ice."

***

"What Pete Morrison said was right, then?" Jennifer said when Chance walked into the ranch house. "Jim really did shoot Tiny?"

"Yup, I'm afraid so, pretty lady. Shot Randy Beuller too, and he's lucky that both men are still alive. I have to ride to Carson City in the morning and report this to Judge Stanfield, Jenny, I guess you know that." He took her in his arms, squeezing tight and kissing her on top of the head.

"Will you find Jim? Will you?" She didn't want Jacob to go, she knew he had to go, and all at the same time, she wanted Jacob to be the one to find and bring Jim Stokes, her only brother, to justice. "We did everything we could to make him right, and he just isn't right, Jacob Chance. You get him, bring him back here to answer for what he's done." Anger and frustration were written across her beautiful face and Jacob took her in his arms again, hugged her tight, and kissed her long and warm.

"Let's go to bed and work on getting Little Jake a sister," he said, gently, taking her by the arms and leading her down the hallway to their bedroom. There were periods of sleep during the night, and they were up well before sunrise.

"It'll take three days to get to Carson City, so just pack some side meat and a few biscuits along with coffee. I'll wear the bearskin coat most of the time, and my heavy boots. You have plenty of wood cut and split, Jenny, and I sent word to Cotton Phelps to keep an eye on things. Buck Colby will be here as well.

"I'll keep you posted on what my plans will be after I see the judge. I'm sure he is going to want me to go after the fool. According to everything we've heard, they have telegraph service all through the northern part of the state, but that won't help me get notes to you."

It took an hour to pack the mule for the long ride, and he stepped into the saddle, kissed Jenny goodbye, and with tears staining their cheeks, he started toward Nevada's capitol city, and the search for her brother, now just a common outlaw.

The storm had abated, but with clear skies came bitter cold. Sunshine during the day melted the top of the snow pack, then overnight froze it solid. "We'll be breaking through this ice the entire trip, Mr. Morgan, so let's go nice and slow." He had some lengths of cloth with him, and after the first hour stopped and wrapped his horse's front legs in the rags.

"There's no way I could ride across the top of the White Mountains," Chance muttered to the big horse. "We'll slip over the top of the hills east and then north. Probably just about the way we'll bring the cattle north, next year," he chortled. "Maybe I'll leave some markers if the trail is a good one."

When they stopped for the day, he pulled the rags from the animals' legs and let them thaw by the fire so they would work again the following morning. He camped under winter-bare skeletons of a grove of aspen trees and had a blazing fire going within minutes. "We're back on the trail, Mr. Morgan, but this is the last time. You are soon to be fully employed as a ranch horse, old man."

***

"You're supposed to be this big old tough guy, Sparks, and look at you, sniveling and cryin' like a baby. So, it's cold. You ain't never been cold? Get your ass away from that fire, get on that set of bones you call a horse, and let's move. You said Ione's just a few hours away. Move it, or I'll shoot you, sure as hell, I will."

Stokes had prodded Thomas most of the late day before, and was on him hard in the morning. After a large fire was started, Sparks Thomas wouldn't move away from it, crying about being frost bit. He finally got started after a heavy boot found its mark, and the two were on the trail, breaking ice covering heavy snow.

"We'll hit the saloon first," Stokes said, nudging his horse into a trot, forcing the animal to go too fast through the drifts. "Just walk in the door and shoot the bartender, then get that bank. We'll be in and out of that town in just a short time. You do it as I say, and we'll be rich, Sparks. Rich."

Chapter Seven

"That's all I know, Gustaf," Jeremy Lawton said when he entered the brewer's hotel room. "That fool Stokes kid shot the bartender and he and Sparks ran. This is not how we planned this. Even though we have spent some of the money, we might be well advised to pull up stakes and get the hell out of here."

"No," Gustaf growled, pacing around the small room, pouring himself a glass of whiskey. "We can still save this. We only wanted Thomas's gun, not his brains," and the two almost choked in their laughter. Gustaf acted like an old man sometimes, but he was only in his early thirties, stocky and arrogant as they come. He poured another and offered the bottle to his partner.

Lawton took the bottle and poured himself a drink, sitting at the small desk. Gustaf continued, thinking as he spoke. "The property is already ours, and we have the maps that I bought that show where Dickson hid his gold. Let's just play it out, build a small brewery and let things calm down."

Following Dickson's death and collapse of the Preston Miller land fraud scheme, word spread through the criminal population that Colonel Dickson had hidden a hoard of gold coins in Preston. There were many, besides Tyrus Watson, having fun with the idea. Gustaf was among many who had actually spent money to buy a purported map of where the money was buried.

Lawton had never voiced the question, but it ran through his mind every time Gustaf brought up the idea of a map. *If the map was real, why isn't the fool selling the map here digging for the gold? Gustaf wouldn't understand the question if I brought it up,* he all but snickered to himself.

"Maybe you're right. That's one hell of a blizzard out there," Lawton said looking out the window at blowing snow, drifting around the buildings on the main street. "At least they won't be catching those fools right away. We have to have some kind of story, in case they bring Thomas back alive. He'll start talking as soon as they slap him around a few times."

"I'm also worried about that, Lawton," Gustaf agreed. "I'm not as worried about these peasants finding out other things." He paced around the hotel room for a few minutes, giving Jeremy Lawton time to pour another draught of whiskey. Gustaf finally stopped his pacing, apparently reaching some kind of conclusion to whatever was bothering him. "If they bring Thomas in alive, you must kill him immediately." Gustaf poured another glass of whiskey and motioned that the conversation was over. "We'll just build a brewery and if Sparks is caught, you will kill him. As soon as this storm is over, we will begin our search along the banks of the river."

"Why are you so sure that so-called map is accurate?" Lawton asked, not understanding the haughty German had concluded the interview. "We heard about several, all different. I think you paid good money for a piece of paper that's a lie."

"No!" Gustaf stormed. "This is the accurate map. I trust Benito. He would not lie to me because he knows I would kill him. Watson told me, this is the real map, and that gold will be mine." He stopped, then said quickly, "Ours."

I'm gonna give this plan of his about two weeks, maybe three, and then I'm gone, Lawton said to himself, leaving the room. *I love gold as much as anyone, but I don't believe in buried treasure. Banks, that's where the*

gold is. Gustaf is mad, and he walked across the icy main
street and slipped into the Crystal Saloon.

***

Jerrod Stockton had two cots set up in the hotel room that
Marcia Whitman made available, each filled with a gunshot
victim, and he had the pleasure of Eileen Sprague's
company. "I worked with the army during the war," she
said, and demanded that Jerrod use her services and
knowledge. "I know gunshot wounds, Mr. Mayor. You
know horses and cattle, I know gunshot wounds."

Stockton wanted to ask, 'which army', but didn't
dare as she held a very sharp knife in her hand. He just
smiled, remembered his Christmas kiss, and let her do her
work.

Eileen Sprague was in her late twenties and
widowed, also a consequence of the War Between the
States. She left Pennsylvania when the war moved close,
then worked as a nurse, moving eventually to Chicago, and
then west, to start a new life as a seamstress. She was
petite, no more than five feet tall, thin as a rail, but with
intense brown eyes and blue-black hair that shone with or
without sunlight.

"My late husband, William Sprague's family was
Germanic, like Gustaf, so I understand the gruff way he
has. I don't like it, one bit, Jerrod, but I understand it. My
family is Italian, back to the days of the Roman Empire, so
don't give me any trouble," and she laughed softly,
reaching out and touching the huge man's shoulder.

She and Stockton were a sight, walking the streets
of Preston, he being a giant at well over six feet tall and
having a bulk of more than two hundred fifty pounds. She
almost had to trot to keep up with his long stride, and
always marveled at his immense strength.

"What will we need that we don't have?" he asked,
putting what few medical instruments he had on the small

hotel table, making sure the water pitcher was full. "I'll keep wood coming for the stove."

"I made a short list," she smiled back, "with the most important things at the top. We'll need to get food over for these two, also. I think Randy Beuller can go home tomorrow, but not until you securely fasten that leg brace. Tiny is gonna be here for a few days."

"I wonder if Marcia knew her hotel would double as a hospital?" he asked, looking over the note. "What's this at the bottom?" He squinted at some very small letters, and read slowly, "I'll roast a goose for our dinner tonight." A broad smile crossed his face and he quickly nodded yes, wanted to hug the lady, wanted another Christmas kiss.

Jerrod Stockton left the hotel, stepped into the still raging storm, on his way to the Sheriff's office and a long talk with Alvarado. With coffee in hand, along with a short squirt from Alvarado's flask, he asked, "Do you think I did wrong bringing that Gustaf to Preston? Chance and Phelps seem to think so."

"How would you know that Gustaf traveled with gunslingers?" the Sheriff answered, as he juiced up his own coffee. "It's cold out there," and he slipped a couple of large chunks of wood into the already red hot stove. "Chance said he had never heard of this Gustaf, and his only question was why build a brewery here when you have one in a town as large as Denver?"

"Marcia Whitman asked me that same question, and so did Cotton Phelps," the blacksmith said. "Well, he's here, he's building a brewery, and one of his partners is involved in shooting two men. What do we do about it?"

"Gustaf hasn't shot anyone, that other fellow, Lawton, looks like he could and would without hesitation, but other than what Stokes and Thomas did, no crime has been committed." He sat back in his old rough wood chair, sipped some hot coffee, and stared at the stove. "I think all we can do is keep a close eye on those two, and hope that they will accidentally let us know what their real plans are."

"I guess you're right," Stockton said, grabbing his basket of supplies. "I better get back to my patients." He made one stop on the way to the hotel, to check on his livery business.

"Mr. Bullis, you look well this morning. I won't be around much for the next couple of days, trying to care for Tiny and Randy. Is there anything you need? Just let me know, and try to keep an eye on those two from Denver. Something tells me there's trouble brewing along with Gustaf's beer."

"Gustaf has a cold heart, Jerrod," Bullis said, "and Lawton's eyes tell me he has killed more than one man. I saw a lot of men become killers in that war, wanton killers, Jerrod, and Lawton has that look in his eyes.

"Yes sir, I'll keep an eye on them. Nobody's been arrested or charged with anything this week, so I won't have to have court, but if somebody gets in trouble I will."

"I know, Roger. I'll cover you if somebody gets dragged into court. I like the idea of Preston having a Justice of the Peace. I'm glad you got elected."

***

"That must have been a rough ride over, Dad. Are you okay?" Jennifer had run into the yard when she saw Ben Stokes ride in through the driving snow and blinding wind of a second major storm. "Come in, quick. Let me get some hot coffee in you," and she had her arms around the old man, helping him into the warm kitchen.

"Just didn't want to be alone, Jenny," he said, slumping into one of the chairs at the dinner table. "I feel so bad about Jim, and at the same time I'm so angry at that boy. Is all of this my fault?" He took the large mug of hot coffee, gently blowing on it before taking a sip. She could see age in the man's face for the first time, not the crinkly little lines around the eyes that sparkled when he smiled, but deep creases buried by worry and age, drawn savagely across his brow and near his mouth.

"Was I wrong in the way I raised you children? Your mother was so wrong, running off from us, but was I wrong, raising you to be strong and independent? What went wrong?"

Ben Stokes was boiling with anger at himself, at young Jim, and terrified that the entire matter was his fault, his doing. Tears welled in both their eyes as Jennifer stood behind her father, rubbing his shoulders, wondering what on earth she could say to ease his grief and pain. "Let me bring Little Jake in, Dad. He loves you so much, and he'll help you smile a bit on this cold morning."

Ben moved to the living room and Chance's big rocker sitting near a roaring fireplace. *Jenny and Chance have done a fine job building this home of theirs. What a difference, Jim shooting Tiny Bidwell and Randy Beuller, and Jenny marrying Chance, having a baby, and building this ranch.*

They're both my children, raised in the same home by me, and completely different. What has made Jim want to be mean and ugly? Why is he so different?

His contemplations were interrupted when Jenny popped back in carrying Little Jake. "Here's your Grandpa," she said, handing him down to Ben. Stokes tickled the little guy, letting joyful laughter brighten his gloomy spirits.

They spent the next several hours talking about life, how she had been raised, how he had done so many things for both children, how it was Jim's fault entirely, for being the type of man he became. Ben played with Little Jake, Jennifer showed off Jacob's new reata and her new saddle, and then they got down to how to make their ranches even better than they are.

"The way Chance has with horses, Jenny, you just need to let him breed and train them. He'll have buyers coming from all over the west, you can bet on that. He told me he has sent a couple of letters to some Mexican Vaquero friends of his, to come work here, and that word will spread like a prairie fire in a gale." She saw the light in Ben's eyes as he talked about their ranch, his ranch, and what he saw as their future.

"You and I have our work cut out, building these herds. We can't let some out of work retired marshal do better than we can," he said, laughing for the first time that day. "I like those bulls you brought in, and if we hold back heifers for a couple of years, we'll have hundreds of big healthy steers to take to market every year.

"Hank Adams said Nevada and eastern California are growing by the thousands, and our beef will be needed. I got a load of eastern papers in that last stage run, and all they talk about, back east, is railroads. We could sure use railroads out here."

"That's the one thing wrong with Preston and the Golden Valley," Jennifer said. "We are hundreds of miles from everything. There are no markets even slightly close to us and Preston certainly isn't very big. Everything we do has to be shipped long distances."

"I guess that's why we have to make our product the best there is," he chuckled, going to the stove for another cup of coffee. "I better get back," he said. "Want to be back before dark."

"No," Jennifer said. "You stay here tonight. Have supper with me and Little Jake and we'll get you off nice and early in the morning. We still have half that goose that Jerrod brought us, and we can fix a little picnic inside the house, next to the fire, just like a summer picnic. How's that sound? In fact, you can help me with the evening chores."

The old man smiled, nodded yes, and sat back down. "You're a fine daughter, Jenny. Jacob Chance is a lucky man."

***

Stockton and Eileen Sprague joined Jose Alvarado and his wife, Maria, for breakfast at the café the following morning. "Looks like this new storm isn't willing to give up," Stockton said, watching the snow blow about outside the windows. "Our two patients are feeling better. We're going to get Randy back home this morning, but that bullet wound Tiny has is trying to fester up some."

"I have no problems knowing you're doing your best, Jerrod," Alvarado said. "I wanted to ride out and follow Stokes' trail this morning, but it won't exist with all this snow. It was hard to see when we were right on it.

"Have you heard anything from our strangers?"

"They've been doing some measuring work, but the storm isn't helping them either. Just being around town is all I've seen," Jerrod answered.

"They walked by my store several times yesterday," Eileen said, "seemed to be looking for something. I didn't talk to either one. That Gustaf can be awfully curt with his talk."

"According to one of Juanito's friends," Maria chimed in, "they were down by the river taking measurements, too. Not where Colonel Dickson got his water. Downstream several hundred feet."

"That's interesting," Stockton said. "There aren't any ditches or outlets down there. Wonder what that might be all about?"

"I'll be making my rounds shortly," the sheriff said, "and I'll make sure I ride through that area. Jerrod, can you kind of spread the word, quiet like, to let people know that we want to know what those two men are doing, where they are doing it, and even when?"

"I've kinda already got that started," Stockton grinned, taking a big swipe of gravy on a biscuit. "Roger Bullis said Gustaf came by the livery trying to buy some shovels. He sent him to Randy's store. He seems to be very antagonistic with people, all the time. I sure wish I knew more about the man."

Chapter Eight

"That's terrible news, Jacob, but I'm going to make it even worse. Two men fitting the description of young Stokes and his companion, Thomas, rode into Ione, coming from the south, and robbed a saloon, killing one man and wounding another. They headed through the Ione canyon toward the Reese River Valley, and may be headed for Austin."

Judge Stanfield sat back in his large leather bound chair, lit a long cheroot and gave Jacob Chance a hard look. "Did we do wrong? Should I simply have put the boy in prison and be done with it? Damn, but I had hopes for that boy."

"I too, Judge, I too. I wired Major Randall in San Francisco as soon as I got to town, late last night. He'll re-instate me into the Marshal Service, so I'll have open jurisdiction to run the fool down. I know that country like the back of my hand, been through it hundreds of times, have friends throughout the territory, so that little bastard won't get away."

The two men spent the better part of an hour reliving the days that led to the current problem, discussing what a pleasure it was that Nevada was now a state, the thirty-sixth star on the nation's banner, and how well Preston is coming along. "Yes, sir, Judge," Chance smiled, "Jerrod Stockton was elected mayor and has that town organized like a brass band. He's everywhere, all the time, and he's even bringing new business and new people to town regularly.

"I tell you, he's a dynamo. Has the ability to see a problem before it becomes a big problem, and works the kinks out in a fair manner. He's a born leader."

***

"I knew that the minute I met the man," Stanfield said. "Things are looking pretty good for our new state. The mines in Virginia City and Austin are pumping out gold and silver by the ton. Now that that horrible war is over, men and families are streaming into the west, building communities at every opportunity.

"Men like Jerrod Stockton are needed everywhere. Well, I know you're anxious to get back on the trail, Jacob, but check with me before you leave. Just in case further word comes in. I'll send out notices, in the meantime to arrest those two on sight.

"When this is over, I would like to make arrangements to visit Preston again, see what has been taking place in that beautiful little valley. I feel somewhat responsible for the town, you know."

They said their good-byes and Jacob left the courthouse for the short walk to the St. Charles Hotel and an early lunch. He went by the telegraph office on the way and found a message for him from Randall. *Good,* he said, reading the short message. *Full reinstatement, and he wants me to meet with Ira Stone before I leave. Didn't know he was in town.* Instead of early lunch, he made the short walk to the federal building complex to find his old friend.

"Well, well, will you look at that," Stone said when Chance walked into his office. "A real, honest-to-goodness Nevada cowboy graces me with his presence." He charged around his desk and the two went into a bear hug that might have killed an average man. Standing back, Stone said, "You look fine, Jacob, fine."

"So do you, Mr. U.S. Attorney for the State of Nevada. So do you. Did you have to buy your way into this appointment?" he laughed, taking a fun poke at Stone. "You were the one that called U.S. Attorneys every foul name you could think of. They won't prosecute when we bring them the bad guys, they won't accept our evidence or witnesses. You've changed your stripes, my friend."

"They couldn't find anyone to take the job and the Major trapped me in the corrals one night, offered a shot of good Kentucky Bourbon, and, well, here I am." He walked back behind his large desk, motioned for Chance to sit, and made himself comfortable in a big leather wingback chair. "What brings you to the capitol?"

Chance outlined the sad tale of the fall of Jim Stokes, that he was once again in the Marshal Service, and when he would be leaving for the chase. "I'm gonna whup that boy so bad he'll wish he'd never heard my name, Ira. Poor old Ben Stokes is all but a broken man because of that fool.

"God, I wish Jennifer were here. She loves you, Mr. Stone, and she'll cry when I tell her you're here. You could have let me know. You missed one hell of a Christmas dinner at Ben's place. A thousand pounds of meat, I think on four open pits, more pies than you could count, and everything to go with it."

"Damn," was all Ira Stone said, giving the impression his mouth was watering. They talked for another hour and Chance said he had to go. "I'll swing down to Preston come spring, Jacob. Tell Jenny I love her too," and Chance headed for that lunch at the hotel.

***

"I have my Morgan stud, Judge, and a good pack mule. I'll load up at daybreak and head toward the Austin area. Any news to pass along?" Chance had his old Marshal's badge pinned to his shirt under the serape, and would leave the capitol in the morning, if all went well. "If I can't stir up something in Austin or the Reese River area, I'll head north.

"Have they got telegraph lines up in that section of the state? We still don't have any in the Golden Valley."

"Nothing further, Jacob. Good luck, good hunting, my friend. In some areas, there is telegraph service, but it's spotty. Sure wiped out the Pony Express." His eyes narrowed and a grim look came across his broad face. "Bring that boy back to stand in front of my bench. No more namby-pamby with that fool. He's going to prison or the hangman's gallows." It was sad anger that was spread across the judge's face, sad that the boy failed, anger that the he, the judge, let him off.

"I've always believed in giving young people a chance to redeem themselves rather than throwing the book at them, and most do. Most have the spark to live according to the law, and very few turn as bad as this Stokes boy has. You bring him back to me, Jacob. I want to make an example of what happens when you fail."

The morning greeted Chance with bitter cold wind and heavy wet snow when he stepped out from the St. Charles Hotel and headed for the stables to begin the long chase. He spent several hours during the evening trying to plot where the two outlaws might go. "I just don't know that much about this Sparks Thomas," he said several times, working out maps he drew of central and northern Nevada. "Stokes has never been out of Preston as far as I know, so I gotta believe that Thomas will be the leader." He thought about that for a few minutes, and changed his mind, again. *Thomas came to Preston with Gustaf, from Denver. Those fools are just riding and being stupid fools. That will make it harder to find them.*

"Happy New Year, Marshal," the stable boy said when Jacob was packed, saddled and ready for the long journey to Austin, Nevada.

"This is a foul way to start a new year," he mumbled back to the boy, touched his spurs lightly to Mr. Morgan and moved off toward the road leading east. The wind howled and was bitter cold with at least six inches of new snow blowing and drifting, which made the morning equal to Chance's mood. *That boy has no idea what's coming his way,* he thought, moving along the Carson River.

The trail he was following was the emigrant trail used by thousands of gold seekers, and the old Pony Express route across the central part of the state, but with a major winter blizzard exploding across the vast desert, Chance was alone on the trail. The ride was slow, fighting drifts, windblown debris, and a pack mule that would rather be somewhere else. He made the first fifteen or so miles to Dayton, stopped just long enough to swill some hot coffee, and pushed on.

Emigrant trains used the area where Gold Creek emptied into the Carson River to give their animals time to recover from the long trek across Nevada, and a small community grew up. There was another village further up Gold Creek called Johnstown, where many gold seekers lived. It was men from Johnstown that discovered the huge Comstock Lode further up the mountain.

"Well," he muttered late in the afternoon, as he neared a stand of cottonwood trees along the river, "you boys win this round. One tired and cold Mr. Morgan, and one angry, cold, and tired Dopy Long Ears, and I guess we'll make camp." It took some doing but he got a good fire started, had the animals tethered on a long line in good grass they pawed to through the snow, and had a lean-to propped in front of the fire.

With the fire fed, he wrapped himself in a Hudson's Bay blanket and draped a buffalo robe over it and worked his way toward sleep. *Can't help wonder what gets into a man to act the way that fool kid acts. His father gave him a good upbringing, could have had that ranch the government gave him, and doesn't give one damn thought about anything. I had my gun pulled and cocked that night in the hotel. Should have shot the fool,* and his eyes slowly closed, as he allowed sleep to come on in.

The buffalo robe was covered in an inch or so of snow when Chance awoke, and the cold was not aided by high winds. "We'll be riding in cold sunshine today, boys," he said to the animals as he stoked a big fire, waiting for the sun to show itself. Coffee, biscuits and some side meat eaten, animals dressed, he was mounted and on the trail quickly.

He followed along the Carson River, lined with cottonwood trees, watched soldiers marching at Fort Churchill but didn't stop on the way past, and moved quickly through the Lahontan Valley, past some huge sand dunes and along the old Pony Express trail without meeting a single person. It was a long cold day, and he stopped often to adjust the rags he had tied to the animal's front legs. In some places, the crust of hard ice seemed to be an inch thick.

"We should be in Austin in a couple more days boys," he muttered to the animals. In fact he didn't see another person until he reached New Pass Station, a Pony Express station now abandoned for that use, but open as a comfortable stop on the journey.

He had a full meal and a warm bed, and was mounted before sunrise for the easy ride down the mountain, across the Reese River Valley, and up a steep mountain into Austin, a flourishing mining camp, alive with miners, cattle ranchers, and outlaws. He arrived late in the afternoon and made his way directly to the Sheriff's office.

"Afternoon, John" he said, stepping into the office and finding the building warm as toast from a cherry-red potbelly stove with a pot of coffee boiling away. "Could smell that coffee half a mile out of town." Two men were in the office, both holding steaming tin cups full.

"Evening to you, stranger," the one behind the desk said. "I'm Sheriff Hildebrand. How can I be of service?" The man was a bear of a man, at least six foot three and probably more than two hundred and fifty pounds, and Chance couldn't see an ounce of fat anywhere.

Chance slipped out of his bearskin coat and flipped his serape over his shoulder, revealing the U.S. Marshal badge. "Good to see you again, Sheriff," he said. "I'm Jacob Chance, U.S. Marshal. We rode together on a manhunt a few years ago. Guess you don't remember. Mind if I thaw out with a cup of that coffee?" He got a friendly nod and poured some into an offered tin cup.

The sheriff stood up, a large smile spreading across his huge face. "I sure do remember, now," he said. "It's been a long time, Chance. This is pretty miserable weather to be out looking over our new state. What brings you to Austin?"

"Two young fools shot up a saloon in Preston, Nevada and then shot up another one in Ione. At least one man is dead and a couple or more are seriously wounded," he said, letting his hands warm up around the tin cup.

"Had any problems like that here?" He had that first cup of coffee down in a flash and poured a second, when the sheriff produced a flask and offered it, which he took with a welcome smile and topped his cup. "Mighty fine, Sheriff. Mighty fine."

Sheriff Hildebrand poured himself a little out of that flask, as well, challenging his cane chair. "I've got three men trying to catch those two right now, Marshal. Tried to rob the bank two days ago, but the clerk chased 'em off with a shotgun blast. Thinks he hit one of them. Had a big storm come through and can't tell you even where my deputies might be right now.

"You say they came up here from Ione? That pretty much means they would be heading north along the Reese River on leaving here. Sure wouldn't go back to Ione. Telegraph lines have been down for a couple of weeks. Damn Indians think it's fun to light the poles on fire when they're all liquored up. I didn't know about the Ione thing."

They talked for several minutes, and Hildebrand offered little. "My deputies are out of town, so until they get back, it's just me and old Tom here. You can get some information from the banker, but he's been pretty cranky."

"Thanks, John," Chance said. "I'll probably be moving out in the morning, but I'll check with you before I leave in case your men get back."

Chance took his animals to the stables, found a room at the International Hotel and sauntered his way through the steep streets of Austin to the bank, which was closing for the day. "Need to talk to the clerk that shot at the men during the attempted robbery the other day," he said, flashing his badge. The manager frowned his displeasure at being delayed in closing, but ushered Chance into the building.

"Mr. Bryson," he called. "Someone here to see you. Meet me in my office. Come along, Marshal, he'll be with you in a moment," and ushered him into a well-appointed office. "Nasty business, bank robbery," the banker said, sitting behind his large oak desk. "Mr. Bryson keeps that shotgun of his at the ready at all times. We've never lost a dime of our client's money, sir. Not a dime." He was proud as a rooster, lighting a cigar, not offering one to Chance, and smiling as Bryson came in.

"This is a marshal wants to talk to you about that robbery, Bryson. Be quick so we can get out of here."

Chance gave the young man a full introduction, glaring at the impudent banker, and pulling a cheroot for himself, offering one to Bryson. "The two men who tried to rob the bank may be the ones I've been following. If so, they are known killers, Mr. Bryson, so you took quite a chance drawing down on them. I'd consider you a lucky feller, right now. Can you give me a description?" When he said, 'known killers,' he looked at the banker to see if there was any affect, and there was, bringing a quick little smile to Chance's face.

The clerk described big Jim Stokes and Sparks Thomas and said the blast from the scattergun may have hit the one he described as Thomas. "I saw him limping a bit when he jumped on his horse, and reaching down to his right leg as they rode out of town. I sure hope I did," he smiled.

Chance looked over at the seated banker and asked, "Is this a federal bank or a state bank?"

"Because of the mines, we're federal," he answered. "Why?"

"Because, sir, the attempted robbery has now become a federal offense, with weapons involved. Makes my job a little bit easier." He thanked Bryson for his information and headed back to his hotel and stopped at the front desk.

"The sheriff said the telegraph lines are down between here and Ione. Are they down everywhere?"

"No, Marshal. We still have a good line west. Goes to Virginia City, Carson City, and all the way to Sacramento. Something I can help you with? The office is right next door."

"I'll take care of it, thank you," he said, stepping out the door and walking to the wire office. He sent two messages, one to Major Randall, one to Ira Stone. He was at the hotel's dining room for supper when the sheriff came in and joined him.

"My men lost the trail in the heavy snow, Marshal, sorry to say. They said it looks like those two might be heading to Dun Glenn or Winnemucca."

"Any indication that one might be wounded?" Chance asked. "Mr. Bryson seemed pretty sure that he hit one of them in the leg."

"I asked that same question and they said they couldn't tell. There is no way they would have seen blood splotches or anything like that in those drifts. What's your plan?"

"I'll be leaving at first light," he said. "But first, a piece of that apple pie, a full pot of coffee, and my last night under warm blankets for awhile." They chuckled over that, and the sheriff joined him in pie and coffee.

"There are two ways they could go," Chance said, sipping some hot coffee. "They could go north, following the Reese River, and north along the mountains toward Dun Glenn and Winnemucca. They did not go west or I would have run into them coming into town. Stokes doesn't have any idea of this country, but I don't know anything about Thomas.

"Have you ever dealt with the man or have any background on him?"

"When you left earlier, I went through all my wanted broad sheets and that name was not there. This might just be two kids got all liquored up," the sheriff said, but knew better as soon as the words were out.

"No," Chance said. "Stokes has been building toward this for a couple of years. He was a dumb, swaggering kid two weeks ago. Right now he's wanted for murder and robbery, and an outlaw with one pissed off marshal on his tail.

"I'm going to take the Dun Glenn trail, probably. If you get any information, forward it to the sheriff in Winnemucca. It's been a pleasure seeing you, and if you get down Preston way, the coffee pot's always hot and full."

They shook hands and Chance headed for his room for his last warm night in a bed.

Chapter Nine

"You been nothin' but a crybaby ever since we got run out of Austin," big Jim Stokes was screaming at Sparks Thomas, as Thomas moaned in pain, curled up in a blanket next to a fire. "Your only job was to walk in the front door of that bank and shoot the teller, but, oh, no, you hesitated just like the coward you are. You let that fool get the jump on us and we had to run, and now you're just a damn little boy cryin' over a little scrape on a leg."

The leg wound was far more than a scrape, had been bleeding for two days, and the pain came from the wound itself along with complications that may have included gangrene. Both men had ridden in bitter cold, with the possibility of frostbite starting to take effect. Thomas had been in and out of consciousness for the last several hours and Stokes wouldn't let up on him.

"We could have robbed the mine office in Ione, not just the saloon if you hadn't got all coward on me and made me shoot the guy in the saloon. Just walk in the door and shoot the son of a bitch, I said, and you said 'put your hands up'. You cost me hundreds of dollars," and he walked over and kicked him in the head. "I hope you bleed to death," he screamed, kicking snow and ice, stomping around the camp area.

"I'm going to rob banks, rob mines and miners, and you're gonna die like the coward you are. My name will be in all the newspapers around the world, and no one will even know you've ever been along. Die," he howled, kicking the unconscious man again.

***

First light found Stokes saddled and extra gear tied to Thomas's horse, Thomas still in his blanket near a fire that was barely smoldering. "Rot, you coward," was all Stokes said as he rode out. "I'll just follow along this long valley and it has to lead me somewhere," he muttered, riding north toward Winnemucca in Humboldt County, but not having any idea where he was going. Hunger was his only companion on the long ride, that and a bitter cold wind.

When the two rode into Austin, before hitting the bank, they bought some cured meat and hard tack biscuits at the hotel, and Stokes had taken Thomas's share as soon as the man passed out that first night. He pulled the trick of a dumb pilgrim, and ate all the meat the second day. He was gnawing on a piece of hard tack and couldn't wash it down with water because his canteen was frozen solid.

"At least I got a few dollars from that old saloon, and Thomas had money I didn't know about. He was holding out on his partner. Die, you bastard," he spat with a wad of tobacco juice, putting his horse into a fast trot, breaking trail through about two feet of snow that carried an ice crust from a full day of sunshine. One thing that was obvious, he learned nothing about horses from his father. With every step, his horse had to break through the heavy crust, and most horses come up lame with serious lacerations and sometimes heavy bleeding.

Stokes didn't slow to let his horses blow, catch their breath, didn't stop for a break for himself, just kept pushing through deep crusted drifts. The wind chill brought the temperature well below zero, despite the sunshine.

***

Chance took the trail that would eventually take him to Dun Glenn and Winnemucca, and after about ten hours of slow travel he pulled Mr. Morgan and the mule to a stop, under a rock outcrop. *I've been breaking fresh trail all day,* he thought, *and Stokes has at least a two-day head start on me. If one of them is hurt and bleeding, now that this storm has passed, I might see something tomorrow.* He snickered, and said out loud, this time, "That is, if they even came this way."

The long north south valley was covered in a white blanket with stars blinking brightly in the cold air as Chance moved around finding some wood, tearing up sage brush, and needing a warm fire. "It's gonna be one cold night tonight," he muttered, stomping his feet to get some warmth flowing.

"Looks like a little grass for you guys if you kick the snow out of the way," he said, unpacking the mule first, then undressing the big Morgan stud. "A nice fire in front of these rocks should keep me warm for a few hours."

He had a pot of coffee, some jerked venison boiled right along in it, and swimming in the red eye gravy that it became. Sopped up with a couple of biscuits he bought at the hotel café, he had no trouble falling asleep. There was just a hint of light when he rolled out, stirred the fire, made a pot of coffee, and prepared for another long hard day on the trail.

Two years off the trail and I'm getting' a bit soft, he snickered to himself, shaking from the cold as he stoked the fire. *I was on the trail, sleeping in dirt, mud, rocks, and ice most of my life, and all I want right now is to be in my own bed, snuggled under several blankets, with my arms around my wife. Stokes, you are looking at one pissed off brother-in-law, when I find you.*

It was close to mid-day when he stumbled onto the tracks of two horses, and when he stepped off Mr. Morgan to take a close look, found a few spatters of blood in the crusty snow. "I've got you now, Mr. Stokes, and you're gonna pay for making Judge Stanfield look bad, for shooting Tiny Bidwell, and for killing that man in Ione. You are gonna pay big time."

He was looking closely at the blood spatters, and then saw what he didn't want to see. "There is blood from a possible gunshot wound there," he said, crouching down, "but this blood looks like it's been splashed from one of the horses. Those fools are breaking through this ice at a fast trot. Horse whipped would be my answer, and may just be when I catch the bastards."

He remounted and moved off at a walk, glaring at the blood in the snow. *I can't believe that Stokes is actually Ben's son. He was just a child when Ben moved his family west, was raised on that ranch, raised in the saddle, and treats a horse this way.* He took that moment to promise that Little Jake would be raised to love and honor, not just horses, but all animals.

Stokes and Thomas had not taken any steps to hide their trail, simply following along a worn path, and Chance made fair time, using their trail and not having to break through the icy snow. "Looks like a camp up there, 'bout half a mile, Mr. Morgan. Let's slow down and keep an eye on things." He had to snicker to himself, knowing that he had talked to his horse all his life, and when he started moving cattle with Jennifer, it drove her nuts. She was always saying, "What'd you say?" and he'd have to tell her he was just talking to his horse.

"Does he talk back?" she quipped, shaking her head, but smiling.

"I know what he's thinking and saying," Chance said. "Right now, even, he's wondering why you don't talk to your horse." She just laughed every time the conversation took place.

"Well?" he continued. "You talk to the cows."

***

Several hundred yards from what looked like a camp, Chance held the horse and mule and moved off the trail. He tied them off and with rifle in hand slowly advanced on the site. *Fire's out,* he noticed, moving through the snow covered sagebrush. *What is that next to the fire? Not moving and I don't see any animals. Maybe they spotted me coming and hightailed it out, leaving something.*

He kept looking at what seemed to be blankets piled near the cold fire pit, and slowly crept up to it. He nudged it with the barrel of his rifle and it seemed solid. When there was no reaction from the bundle, and he saw no animals or people, he knelt down and opened the blankets. Sparks Thomas's body was frozen solid in the near zero temperature.

Looks like that bank teller did his job, Chance muttered, *and Mr. Stokes is now alone. Ben told me that boy had never been outside Preston; I wonder where he thinks he's going?* Chance spent the next hour doing what he could to build a cairn for Thomas's body, to try to protect it from critters, and by the middle of the afternoon, was back on the trail.

"It's not hard to follow this fool, is it Mr. Morgan. He's riding that horse way too fast for these conditions. If he keeps it up, I'll have him in custody by this time tomorrow. That horse will be lame in no time." As the late afternoon, mid-winter light began to fail; Chance started looking for a decent place to camp. "You boys need some good grass and I need to stay a little warm. My bones are getting older, Mr. Morgan, Sir," he said, moving off the trail and toward a stand of cottonwood trees.

With good grass for the animals under the blanket of snow and plenty of wood for a fire, Chance had a good camp, ate well, and was ready for a warm sleep. He watched the stars dance in the frigid sky, heard coyotes singing mournful tunes across the broad valley, and just before letting his eyes close, said goodnight to Jennifer and Little Jake.

Chance was back on the trail before the sun peeked over the eastern hills after warming himself with a big fire and a pot full of coffee, mixed with some meat and hard tack. He found a camp not far from where he camped, which told him a big story. *That boy's horse is giving him hell,* he said, stepping off his stud and moving through the campsite.

Looks like one of the horses is bleeding, he noticed, kneeling down to look at a spot of blood. *Probably cut his leg breaking through this ice crust. That kid is a waste. Raised on a cattle and horse ranch and doesn't know the first thing about horses.* He remounted and picked up the trail quickly, and just as quickly found that Stokes had company.

A new set of tracks from two animals joined with those Chance was following, coming in from the west. *I've got four animals and how many riders?* he wondered, getting off the stud and looking at the trail closely. *Stokes is trailing Thomas's horse,* he said to himself, *but it looks like these other two horses each has a rider. That second horse isn't following the same track, so isn't being ponied.*

Before he could catch up with the group they made their way across the pass and dropped down to the Humboldt River and into Winnemucca, a bustling little community right on the immigrant trail. Ranches spread out to the four points of the compass, and enough traffic on the roads that Chance lost the tracks of the group.

"Sheriff, good morning," he said, stepping through the doors into a large office. He slipped out of his bearskin coat and flipped the serape over his shoulder. "I'm Jacob Chance, U.S. Marshal. Need to have a chat. Have coffee?" He had a big hand stretched out and a smile on his face. "Damn cold out there."

"It sure is, Marshal Chance, yes, sir, it sure is cold today. I have coffee, and time for a nice chat." The sheriff was as friendly a man as Chance had met in some time and he looked forward to the next couple of hours, sitting near that potbelly stove and large coffee pot boiling away on top of it.

He told the story again, of the shootings in Preston, the killing in Ione, and the attempted bank robbery in Austin. "Sparks Thomas is dead, so he's out of the picture, but young Stokes is a very dangerous man. He may very well be in your town right now."

"I'm kind of limited on people, Marshal. They keep quitting and running off to the mines. Gold fever can make a feller awful dumb," he snickered. "Why don't you get your animals taken care of and maybe we can take a walk around town, see if that boy is here.

"Seems like the mines up north, in the Jordan Valley, or over in the Boise District would be more to his liking."

"That would probably be true except for one thing. That fool boy has never been out of Preston. He wouldn't know Jordan Valley from Carson City. I'll catch up with you shortly," Chance said, and headed out to take his animals to the stables.

***

"Thanks for riding with me, boys. You're good company and I'll do as you say and get the horses legs patched up right away. Have a good trip. You say I can get into the Jordan Creek mining district and even the Snake River mines at Boise just by going north toward Paradise Valley?

"That's really good to know." Stokes watched as the two cowboys rode off toward a ranch somewhere east of town. *Little bastards, trying to tell me how to take care of horses. They don't know who they're dealing with. Should have just shot the fools and taken their money.* He walked his horses through Winnemucca, saw the bank, and it was right on the road that led toward Paradise Valley, and a block or two past that were stables next to a hotel.

Those two mining areas must be filled with money. Banks, gambling halls, stupid miners with their pockets full of gold. That would be an area ripe for pickin'. I gotta think on that for a spell, Stokes thought, walking his horses toward the livery, eyeing the bank as he passed.

The livery owner didn't say anything but wanted to. *That boy should be whipped bringing me horses that look like this,* he thought, cleaning the deep cuts and wounds on the legs of both horses suffered from breaking through heavy ice on the trail into town. *Oh, oh,* Hans Kelsey saw blood that did not come from either horse. *Blood all over the stirrup and fender-skirt,* he said to himself. *Somebody riding this horse was bleeding heavy. I need to tell the sheriff.*

He was finishing treating the horses' legs when another rider stopped in front of the stables and stepped off his horse. He was trailing a well-packed mule. "Morning," he said, leading the animals into the barn. Chance spotted the two injured animals immediately. "Nasty wounds, there. Looks like someone was breaking ice in a hurry to get here. Mind if I take a look?"

"Be quick about it," Kelsey said. "I have to report this to the sheriff."

Chance produced his badge and said, "Just report it to me, sir. I'm Jacob Chance, U.S. Marshal, and I've been trailing the man with these horses for three days now."

"U.S. Marshal, eh? Look at the blood here," and he pulled the stirrup up for Chance to see. "Here too," and he pointed out the blood on the fender-skirt. "Somebody was bleeding bad."

"I buried that somebody yesterday, Smithy, a bank robber, and the man that brought these horses in was his partner. Which way did he go?"

"Looked like he was heading to the hotel, or maybe that saloon next to it." Kelsey paused for just a minute. "He asked how far it was to Jordan Valley. Thought you might want to know."

Chance smiled, hearing that. "You go tell the sheriff what you found, that you met me, and tell him I might need help at either the hotel or the saloon," Chance said, making fast the lead ropes for the stud and mule. *So that fool wants to head north, has no plan, and now has no partner, and is about to lose his horses. Jim Stokes, you are the biggest fool I've met in a long time. I'm gonna drag your butt through the middle of Preston when I get you back there.* Chance was scowling, thinking of Tiny Bidwell, Judge Stanfield, and most of all, old Ben Stokes. *Jennifer will have her hands full, taking care of Little Jake and her father. I'm gonna whup that boy bad when I find him.*

Thinking of Jennifer and Little Jake brought a smile to his face. *This is exactly why I quit the Service,* he said to himself. *My responsibility should be to my wife and child, not chasing some damn fool across the state. If it was any other damn fool, I'd let somebody else chase him, but I also have a responsibility to Ben. Damn that boy.*

***

Kelsey scurried up the street toward the sheriff's office and Chance slipped out of his bearskin coat and tied it to the back of his saddle, brought the rifle out and walked toward the hotel. "Need a room for a night or two," he smiled to the clerk, pulling the registration book over. "How much would that be?" He scanned the registration and found no one had checked in.

"Be two dollars, and that includes one bath. The shave is another twenty-five cents."

"Need all of it," Chance chuckled, offering a five dollar gold piece and rubbing the stubble on his chin. "Where's some good hot food? Been on the trail and I ain't the best cook."

"The saloon's there," and he pointed next door, "and right across the street is a fine restaurant. An old Basque lady runs the place, and she can cook."

"Thanks," Chance said. "I'll be back after I get something hot in my belly to pick up the key and get that bath and shave." He walked out the door in time to meet the sheriff hurrying down the street.

***

"Stokes didn't register at the hotel," he told Sheriff Sanford. "He might be in the saloon there. The blood on the stirrups just about confirms that those horses were brought in by Stokes."

They walked toward the saloon, each carrying a rifle. The building stood between two other buildings and was substantial, made of brick and stone, with large windows that looked out on the main street. The entrance was typical, consisting of double bat-wing doors. "There's a back door," Sanford said. "I'll come in that way. Wait 'till you see me come in before coming through the swinging doors. If he's there, he'll be trapped." The sheriff started toward the alley-way between the buildings.

"He's shot three men, Sheriff, so don't take any chances," and Chance moved toward the window of the saloon to watch for Sanford's appearance. *Too dark in there to see if he's there,* Chance thought, peering through the filthy glass. Within a couple of minutes, he caught a glimpse of Sanford as he walked through a door in the back of the saloon. Chance moved to the bat-wing doors and walked in, rifle at the ready.

Patrons saw the sheriff come in the back door, rifle cocked and ready, then saw a man in a floppy sombrero and serape, big badge showing come in the front door. The saloon got very quiet instantly. "Stokes, you in here?" Chance bellowed, stalking down the long bar, looking at each man while the sheriff moved through the various tables scattered around the large room.

Some men, particularly the ones at the tables, tried to duck their heads, so as to not be recognized. Sanford used his rifle to lift their heads, but Stokes was not in the building.

Before they were finished with their search, gunfire was heard down the street. Everyone scrambled for the front doors and Chance and Sheriff Sanford had a hard time shoving their way through the crowd. "Coming from the bank," someone yelled as more gunfire could be heard.

Sanford and Chance were running with a crowd of men down the main east-west thoroughfare. There was scattered gunfire, to the north this time, close to the Humboldt River. As they neared the bank building, the crowd separated allowing the two lawmen to come through. Two bodies were sprawled across the board sidewalk, and inside, they found another man shot dead, and one wounded, shot through the leg.

"It was horrible, Sheriff," Bank Manager Jefferson said, wiping sweat from his brow despite the cold temperatures. The very overweight man was more than distraught, Chance thought, watching him pace about as he spoke. "He walked through the door, shot the only customer at the teller's cage, then shot my clerk Hanson in the head, leaped the counter and stuffed all the money in a bag, took a shot at me, and hightailed it out the door, where, I guess, he shot those two out there. Horrible, it was just horrible."

Jefferson had to sit down, his hands shaking, still sweating profusely, his fat jowls actually dripping. "Was he a young man, pencil moustache, bright blue eyes?" Chance asked, standing over the manager.

"Yes," he answered, "and with several day's beard. He was dirty, and seemed extremely angry. I'm sure I've never seen him before."

Chance and Sanford walked quickly back to the stables, ignoring the hundreds of questions aimed at them from those brought out by the gunfire. "The boy's horses are at the stables, Sheriff, so he must have run down that street to the north and stolen a horse. That was probably the second bunch of shots we heard."

"You give chase, Marshal," Sanford said. "I'm going to put a posse together and we'll catch up with you. I think you're dealing with someone who might be mentally insane."

Chance was willing to agree with the sheriff, and saddled his Morgan stud and packed the mule quickly. When he rode onto the north road, he found a small crowd around a badly wounded man. "I'm U.S. Marshal Jacob Chance," he said to a man tending the wounded man. "Sheriff Sanford will be along shortly. Tell me what happened, and don't waste words," he said.

"Man just ran down the street and shot old Charley, right off his horse, jumped on the horse and raced out of town, that way," and he pointed north. "Charley got off a couple of shots, but I don't think he hit the bastard."

"Thanks," Chance said, and turned the horse and mule north, leaving at a trot. The road toward Paradise Valley is well used, connecting with roads going east and west. One road led into Paradise Valley, another crossed the Queen's River and ran through the Black Rock Desert. The main road itself led toward Fort McDermott, an army post built because of Indian problems. The road eventually would lead into Oregon, connecting to main roads into Idaho.

Trailing that fool isn't going to be easy, Chance thought, seeing so much use on the main road. *If he drives that old man's horse as hard as he did the others, he'll be walking soon.*

He put his animals in a solid trot on the well-used trail, knowing that he would be running out of daylight in just a few hours. "That boy doesn't have anything with him," he chuckled, feeling the cold of the afternoon biting through his bearskin coat. "He has no food, no bedroll, no water. I think he'll actually be glad to see me, when I shove my gun up his nose."

Chance saw massive clouds building to the north and west and knew instinctively that he would be riding into the teeth of another blizzard, if not today, tomorrow for sure. *I don't know what made me buy so much cured meat and hard tack back in Austin, but I'm sure glad I did. I hope this is the biggest damn storm of the century and Stokes gets his stupid self trapped by it.*

Those thoughts helped as he put Mr. Morgan and the ponied mule into a little faster trot, keeping an eye on the storm. "Wind's got a chill to it, Mr. Morgan. We'll need a big fire tonight."

Chapter Ten

Winter chores at the ranch were time consuming and difficult because of cold, heavy snow, and the incredible worry of a sister whose brother was an outlaw and whose father was heart-broken. "I don't know how you were able to handle everything when it was just you and little Georgia," Jennifer Chance said over coffee when Sarah came to visit. "I don't ever want Chance to leave, again. We have three men working for us and I swear, Jacob must have been doing the work of two or three by himself."

"I remember building the house, having Jerrod and Cotton working their butts off and falling into bed before the sun went down more than once. Georgia was barely eight years old when we arrived here in the valley, and she was a handful, too." Sarah walked to the stove and brought the coffee pot back to the table, pouring two cups of steaming energy for them.

"Have you gotten any word at all from Jacob?" Sarah asked, sitting back down. "You must be worried sick."

"He would have to send word by a rider and that isn't going to happen. Anxious? Yes, that is true, but I'm not worried, not about Jacob Chance. I'm worried sick about Jim, though. I can't imagine what got into him to shoot Tiny and then run away. My God, Sarah, he even shot Randy. He must have lost his mind is all I can think."

"Jose Alvarado put up a thousand dollar reward, but I don't think Jim will ever come back to Preston," Sarah said, reaching across the table to take Jennifer's hand. "He was always mean to me and Georgia, tried to keep Cotton from helping me when we got thrown off the ranch by that horrible banker.

"No, Jim will never come back to Preston." The two women sat quietly, wondering what might be in store for the young man should Jacob Chance track him down. "Would Jacob bring him back to Preston?" Sarah finally asked.

"No," Jennifer answered quickly. "Chance said he would take him straight to Judge Stanfield in Carson City. What have you heard about the man that rode off with Jim after Tiny got shot?"

"Cotton said that three men came to town to open a brewery and he was one of them, a real jerk is the way Cotton described him. Jerrod came out yesterday to talk to Cotton about goose hunting again, and said a man named Gustaf was the brewer but that no work had been done. He thinks the men are up to something but doesn't know what.

"I better be getting back to the ranch. Georgia's supposed to be helping Cotton and they'll be getting on each other's nerves by now. She teases him and he teases her, and then no work gets done," she said, the two laughing at the thought.

"She sure has grown up," Jennifer said, helping Sarah into her winter coat. "Do you ever have any trouble with that leg you broke?"

"I can feel it once in a while, but it never hurts or gives me trouble. Thanks for the coffee and talk. Come by our place, will you?"

"I will," Jennifer said. "I've been awfully busy here and trying to take care of Dad, too. He's really hurting, and still blames himself for Jim's stupidity. I can't get him out of that."

Sarah mounted up and rode back toward her ranch and Jennifer went back into the big house to get Little Jake up from his nap. "Come on, big boy, let's get you all bundled up against old man winter and go check on those cows and horses. Sure be glad when you learn to walk better," she laughed, then remembered all the stories she's heard about the terrible twos and children getting into everything. "Just crawl," she snickered, "Until your father gets home."

***

"Ah, Sheriff, I've been looking for you." Gustaf came into the sheriff's office with muddy boots, pants covered in mud, and a face full of anger. "Mr. Lawton and I were down along the Good Hope River, looking for a second or possibly third source of water for my brewery when I was accosted by one of your citizens."

"Oh?" Jose Alvarado said, looking up from some paperwork spread across his desk. "Pray tell, Mr. Gustaf, tell me about this." There was no smile, and Alvarado was in no mood for idiots on a cold blustery morning. "You wouldn't have been on private property in your search, by chance?"

"The river is not private property, for one thing, and Mrs. Whitman may own the hotel but she does not own the river. She attempted to strike me with a willow branch, and I want her arrested immediately."

"Mr. Gustaf, this is the third day in a row you have come to my office, tracking mud each time, to tell me that some land owner has chased you off their property. I'm not sure what you think you're doing, but you have access to the river from the property you own. If I get one more complaint from a landowner about your trespassing, I will file the necessary charges and you will stand before the justice of the peace.

"I hope you understand this. There has been trouble in this town before with people not recognizing property rights, Mr. Gustaf, so heed my warning. Good day, sir," Alvarado said, turning back to his paperwork.

Gustaf stood stock still for just a moment, then turned quickly and left the office, stomping a bit of mud on the way out. "That was childish," the sheriff murmured, smiling as he watched the door close. He couldn't concentrate on trying to work out the finances of the office and put the papers aside, pulling on his heavy winter coat and grabbing his hat. "Maybe time for a chat with Jerrod Stockton."

Gustaf stormed up the muddy street toward the hotel, to find Lawton, and caught a glimpse of him in the café. "Jeremy," he said, too loudly, as he plopped himself at Lawton's table. "I think we need to make some changes in our plans. When you have finished your meal, join me at the stables."

"Actually, I'm just having coffee, Gustaf. We can go now," and he stood up, gathering his heavy winter coat. "What kind of change are you thinking? It seems that everyone in town is angry at us, and with you insisting on getting onto private property, we won't be able to find that hoard, if there even is one."

"We were told that Colonel Dickson hid that gold along the banks of the river, right in town, Jeremy," Gustaf snarled in his guttural manner, almost looking down the length of his nose at his partner. "I don't believe we were lied to, and I will find it."

"Assuming we were not lied to," Lawton came back, "it is possible that someone has already found the gold, or that Dickson did not bury it after all. Remember, Gustaf, his partner was a banker, with a bank vault. I've questioned this idea from the beginning, and still do."

"There is a way to find out if someone else has already found that iron box full of gold. I think it's time to get rough, Jeremy. I think we should kidnap a hostage and demand that the gold be given to us.

"I'm going to make one more attempt to locate the buried gold this afternoon, and if I can't find it, we need to make plans to force these people to give us the gold." They continued their walk through town to the stables.

"That's wrong, Gustaf, very wrong. If Dickson hid money and it's been found, what makes you think whoever found it has said anything? Or is even still in town? You have gold on the brain, and I'm about to pull out of this mess you've created." Lawton was a gunslinger, but couldn't see himself as a kidnapper or hostage taker.

I'm only going so far in these plans of his, and no farther. He's mad, and that could get me killed. You better be very careful, Gustaf, Lawton was thinking, glaring at the man. *I'll listen to this new plan, but I'm not going to kidnap anyone.*

"You are getting paid by me, Lawton," Gustaf growled, increasing his swagger with each step. "There is gold, and it will be mine. You'll get your share, just as we have said, but you will do as I say.

"Take a horse ride, Jeremy, and find someplace where we can hide our hostage while we make our demands."

Lawton nodded, and walked into the large barn and blacksmith shop while Gustaf turned and headed back into the heart of Preston. Lawton watched him walk away, stepped into the livery office to talk about a horse with Jerrod Stockton's new hand, Roger Bullis.

"Were you here when all the problems with Dickson and Miller took place?" he asked the justice of the peace. "I'd sure like to know more about this Colonel Dickson."

"No," Bullis answered, sitting at the desk, enjoying the warmth from a large potbelly stove. "I've only been in town a short time. If you want to know about those two you should talk with Jerrod Stockton. He still carries a massive hate for both of them.

"Why do you ask?"

"I was just wondering. There are so many rumors about gold being hidden by Dickson," Lawton answered. "Well, if he hid gold, somebody has probably already found it. I need to rent a good trail horse, Bullis. Want to look at some land around these parts," he lied.

"I guess we've all heard enough stories and lies about Dickson. He was a gangster and killer, but I don't think I've heard any good stories about burying gold. Hell, his partner owned a bank," Bullis laughed. "Come on, I'll get you a good riding horse."

***

Alvarado was hailed by Marcia Whitman as he walked toward the Crystal Saloon, hoping to find Stockton. "Hello, Mrs. Whitman. Gustaf just told me that you gave him a willow switch whippin'. I imagine he deserved it," the sheriff chuckled.

"He did indeed, Sheriff Alvarado. He did indeed," she said, and without benefit of a smile or chuckle. "I need some legal advice if you have a minute or two."

They went inside the hotel and to Whitman's little office in the back. There was a nice fire going in a wood stove, and a pot of water boiling on top. "I don't have coffee, Sheriff, but I mix a fine cup of tea. Will you join me?"

Alvarado nodded thank you and pulled a chair up to her desk. "What kind of legal problem would you have?"

"I want those two men out of my hotel, Sheriff. They are filthy in their rooms, they dig holes in my little garden near the river, they are surly toward those who work for me, but they pay for their rooms. How can I throw them out?"

"I don't see where they have broken a law, Mrs. Whitman, with the exception of trespassing along the river. I have had a bad feeling about the men from the day they rode into town, but except for their trespassing, they haven't done anything wrong.

"Have they broken furniture or windows? Have they assaulted you or one of your employees? Unless they break the law, there isn't anything I can do, I'm afraid."

She and Alvarado talked for another ten minutes or so without reaching any kind of decision on how to handle Gustaf and Lawton. "I'm going to be meeting with Jerrod Stockton in just a few minutes, Marcia," Alvarado said. "Maybe he can come up with some ideas. He has a great distaste for that Gustaf, and more so, knowing he invited the man to open a business in Preston."

***

Alvarado and Mayor Stockton had Chance's old "office" table at the back of the Crystal Saloon, a couple of large schooners of beer in front of them. "Gustaf and Lawton have been chased off at least four different properties along the river, so far," Alvarado said. "This morning, Marcia chased the man off with a willow switch," he said, chuckling at the thought. "Somebody's going to get hurt if this continues.

"Marcia wants to throw them out of the hotel, but they haven't done anything that would justify her doing that. I'm sure she can't unless they break something or hurt someone, or break the law in some way."

"Maybe I'll just get in a fight with that German fool. He better not try to hurt Mrs. Whitman," Stockton said, an angry look in his face. "I have come to dislike that man and would take pleasure busting his face.

"And, damn it, Jose, you're right. We can't do anything until they break a real law. Trespass is one thing, but they will have to break a serious law."

"I told Gustaf that just one more trespass complaint and charges would be filed," Alvarado said. "I wish I knew what it was they were doing. They tell me they're looking for another river source for brewing water, but that's a lie.

They have a fine pipeline already in place, and we know how good the beer was from Colonel Dickson."

"Tiny Bidwell is home now and we were talking about that last night. That Sparks Thomas fool who ran off with Jim Stokes was talking about a map of some kind that Gustaf had with him. You don't suppose that Dickson and Miller hid money or gold somewhere, do you? That might account for some of this."

Alvarado sat back, thinking hard on what Stockton just said. "You remember that I was one of those who cleaned up the mess when Dickson's saloon burned to the ground. We came up with an awful lot of gold coins, some partially melted, and burned money. At the time, I wondered why there was so much gold when Dickson's partner owned a bank.

"Maybe there was no trust between the two, and Dickson would be the type to bury money somewhere. Not in town, right along the river, though."

The conversation came to an end with gunfire at the south end of town. Both men hit the street at a full run, toward Randy Beuller's store. A small crowd had already gathered behind the building, along the riverbank, by the time they got there. "What's going on," the sheriff said as men and women parted for him to pass through.

Beuller was on the ground, bleeding from a wound to his good leg, the other still in a splint. "Gustaf," was all he said before passing out. Stockton had a couple of men help him into his home at the back of the store.

"Did anyone see this?" Alvarado asked, looking around at the crowd.

"Randy's wife came into the store," Eileen Sprague said, "and told him that Gustaf was digging near the river. He went out to see what was going on, and then we heard the shot. Is he going to be okay?"

"Jerrod will take care of him," the sheriff answered, moving toward the river, finding a shovel and pick near a small hole in the ground. He was about to move back onto the main street when Roger Bullis from the livery stable came at a hobbled trot to the back. His war wounds would never fully heal, and the pain from trying to do heavy work was intense. Running from the livery to Beuller's store was more than intense.

"There's trouble at the hotel, Sheriff," Roger panted. "Better get up there."

"Let's go," is all he said, and he started running up the street toward the hotel. "What has that fool done now?" he panted, sloshing through the snow, ice, and mud.

Bullis and several men trailed well behind, and joined the sheriff in front of the hotel. Bullis was panting and whimpering slightly from the pain. "I heard Mrs. Whitman yelling at someone, she was very angry, and then I heard what sounded like furniture breaking, and someone was screaming. I'm not a well man, Sheriff, and I can't fight because of my old wounds."

"You did the right thing," the sheriff said, looking at the front of the hotel. "You men stay out here, and come in only if I call." Alvarado had his revolver in hand and burst through the front door to find broken chairs, one table upside down, and a kerosene lantern broken. Luckily it had not been lit. As he looked around, he spotted a blood trail down the long hallway toward the back of the building. He sprinted back to the street.

"Go get Stockton and have him meet me behind the hotel. Hurry, Roger, hurry," the sheriff said, slipping back into the lobby. He slowly walked along the hallway, his weapon cocked and ready and saw blood spatters leading out the back door. He was very cautious before stepping out into the cold winter afternoon.

A small crowd was beginning to gather and Alvarado motioned for people to stand back. "Looks like whoever did this had a couple of horses tethered back here," he said when Jerrod Stockton arrived. "I'm afraid

Marcia Whitman may have been abducted, Jerrod, and from the amount of blood, either she or her abductor may be seriously injured as well."

Alvarado turned to the crowd of men and women. "I would like at least three of you men to ride with me. Get your horses and we'll leave from right here in ten minutes. Jerrod, can you ride with me? Is Randy okay?"

"Randy is far more angry than he is injured, Jose. His wife and Eileen are taking good care of him. I can ride with you, gladly. Do you think it was Lawton or Gustaf that did this?"

"Certainly seems logical, Jerrod. Gustaf shot Randy and within minutes someone kidnaps Marcia, but only two horses were tied off back here. That means that either Lawton or Gustaf may still be in town."

"No," Bullis said. "Lawton rented a horse several hours ago and rode out of town. Gustaf has kept two horses for himself since they arrived, paying full price each day for them. It must have been Gustaf that kidnapped Marcia."

"Well, this proves you were right, Jerrod," Alvarado said with a wry smile. "You said I need a full time deputy, and if I had one, this might not have happened. Well, that's to come, let's get our horses."

***

"You are a stupid man, Mr. Lawton. A very stupid man."

"Don't start that with me, Gustaf. You said, we need a hostage to get that money. Looks like you got a hostage, and you wanted me to find a place for us to hide. Well, this looks pretty hidden to me.

"And a sheriff, and a posse, and some angry townspeople are probably on their way. In the middle of the day you shot a man, then kidnapped the woman. The entire town of Preston will be searching for us, and you call me a stupid man. I should shoot you, myself, and claim the reward. Remember, the sheriff in Denver has a reward out for you."

For his long ride to the buttes north and east of Golden Valley, Lawton had been wondering how to get away from the gold-crazed Gustaf. *If he shows up, I'm just going to shoot the man dead. The sheriff in Denver has a reward for him, I'll have this hick sheriff here verify that I shot the fool and to forward the money, and I'll get as far away from all this stupidity as I can.*

Gustaf was stomping around, kicking rocks, pulling his revolver, putting it back in its holster, kicking more rocks, and finally just standing in front of Lawton, glaring at him. Both men could fully understand that their current position was filled with more than just danger, and both were willing to shoot the other.

"You both will die for this," Marcia Whitman whimpered, sitting in the dirt, dabbing at cuts on her face, and tending to a bad cut on her leg, where a piece of furniture hit her when it was thrown across the hotel lobby. She was about to say something else, but was stopped when Lawton took a wild swing at Gustaf, sending the German brewer tumbling through the rocks and brush.

Gustaf had his revolver out before he stopped rolling in the dirt and fired two quick shots; the first smashing through Lawton's left leg, and the second ripping the man's heart apart. Gustaf slowly got to his feet and pointed the weapon at Mrs. Whitman. "You just say one word, woman. Just one."

He jerked her to her feet and pushed her toward the horses. "Get on," he snarled, nudging her with his revolver and mounting his own horse. Her leg began bleeding again as soon as she mounted the horse. She opened her winter coat and ripped part of her blouse and tried to tie it to the wound.

"You try to run away and you will die. We cross the river and you ride where I ride."

"You're just another filthy killer, Mr. Gustaf, if that really is your name. Sheriff Alvarado will chase you down like the vermin you are, and I'll laugh in your face when he shoots you, laugh harder when I watch you hang."

He raised his arm as if to back hand her across the face, but she nudged her horse out of the way. *You better watch out, Mr. Gustaf,* she said to herself. *You're dealing with one angry woman. I wonder if he knows where we're going? They have been here for a couple of weeks now, but has he made any rides out of town?*

She couldn't remember, but if they continued following the river, she thought, they would soon be coming up on some of the outlying ranches. *He won't want to be seen, and that's to my benefit. I know all the ranchers and he doesn't.*

After half an hour following along the eastern bank of the Good Hope River, Gustaf turned east toward some low lying rocky hills, pocked with box canyons and stands of pine and cedar. Where natural springs came to the surface, cottonwood trees and aspen groves were thick, along with the always present willows.

A few of the narrow canyons actually drifted over and out the other side and into a long valley that ran north and south. It was a dry and harsh environment compared to the lush Golden Valley, and there were no settlers in the area that Marcia Whitman could remember. Her vision was giving her trouble, the pain from the leg wound was intense, and she realized that between the effects of the wound and loss of blood, she might actually pass out.

"Please, Mr. Gustaf," she pleaded, "we must stop. My leg hurts and I feel sick. Do you have water?"

"No stop," he growled, and spurred his horse into a trot. "Keep up or die, woman."

***

"He's not trying to hide his trail at all," Sheriff Alvarado said, as the five men loped on the main road north out of town. They could see the fresh trail in the mud easily, and followed it until it veered sharply toward the river.

"Looks like he crossed the river, Jose. Maybe you could send one of these men up the main trail here to warn the ranchers that Gustaf is on the loose with a hostage."

"Good idea, Jerrod," Alvarado said, and one of the men came forward immediately and volunteered. "Get to Jennifer Chance first," the sheriff said. "Even though she has hands working there, she is vulnerable, then alert as many of the ranches as you can."

With patches of old snow, places filled with melted snow and mud, the trail left by Gustaf and Whitman was easy to follow. "Looks like he might be making for the rocky hills to the east, but if he turns back north, he'll surely come onto one of the ranches up there."

"Sending that rider, Sheriff, should keep folks safe," Stockton said. The two were riding side by side with two riders following. "What's that up there?" Stockton said, pointing. "That a body?" Putting the horses into a gentle lope they rode up on the crumpled body of Jeremy Lawton, face down in the mud.

"Lawton and Gustaf must not have been as tight as we thought, but we now know for sure that Gustaf is as mean a killer as I have been thinking." Sheriff Alvarado was pacing around the area and found a shred of Whitman's blouse. "Marcia's hurt bad, Jerrod, look. She's lost a lot of blood."

The posse moved off at a strong trot, easily following the fresh trail as it moved more and more toward the hills to the east. "If he gets over the top and into that long valley, we'll have to ride hard to ride him down," Alvarado said, touching his horse lightly with his spurs. "It'll be a cold camp tonight, I'm afraid."

Chapter Eleven

Winnemucca Sheriff Sanford and his posse caught up with Chance within the hour. "I'm running out of my jurisdiction, Chance," Sanford said as the riders stopped on the trail. "One of the men from the Paiute tribe that the army uses for scouting is Captain Sou and he heads a squad of Paiute scouts. I have brought Eyes Like Cougar, one of the trackers to ride with you."

"Thank you Sheriff," Chance said, nodding to the tall Indian, "and welcome, Eyes Like Cougar. You're heading back, then, Sheriff? Thank you for your help. If it's possible, I'll try to keep you advised of my situation, and if you could pass that along to Judge Stanfield in Carson City, it would be appreciated. I also left some property at the hotel if you could pick that up and hold it until I return."

"I'll do that, Marshal. Anything else I can help you with?"

"You might wire ahead to Oregon and Idaho officials that Stokes may be headed their way and to treat him as 'most dangerous.' Let's go, Mr. Cougar, we have some serious catching up to do," and he saluted the sheriff, turning his horse and mule back to the trail and leaving at a solid trot.

The road north was generally well used, but with a major blizzard about to descend on them, they were alone on the trail, and the only fresh tracks were those they thought belonged to Stokes. The snow was crunchy but not really deep enough to cause trouble for the horses and mule.

Chance liked what he saw in his new companion. Eyes Like Cougar was tall for a Paiute, heavily built, and dressed in traditional buckskins covered by a heavy wool blanket, tightly wrapped against the winter wind. He had what Chance called searching eyes, set deep in his face.

"Did you get your name from the way your eyes seem to pierce right through whatever you're looking at?" he asked, as they easily followed the trail. "Or do you have exceptional vision?"

"Probably a little of each," Cougar answered in a deep and strong voice. "I've always been a fine hunter, particularly in heavy brush and timber country. You have quite a reputation, Marshal. I've heard your name often."

"Just comes from long service, probably," Chance replied. "Do this kind of work enough, people tend to talk some."

They rode for another half hour, quietly, watching the trail ahead, and keeping a close eye off to the sides as well. They passed a branch that would lead deep into Paradise Valley and over a high pass toward Oregon. Chance and Cougar stayed on the trail that Stokes appeared to follow. It too, continued north toward Oregon, along the western flank of the Santa Rosa Range.

"What are these Indian troubles up north that I've been hearing about?" Chance asked his new trail partner. "Something we should worry about?"

"Probably not, Marshal. Our tribe, under Chief Winnemucca has been friends with white people for many years, helped many when the trails west through the Black Rock Desert were opened, but so much traffic, so many people, have hurt the northern Paiute's, some call them Bannock, and the Pitt River Paiute's ability to hunt and provide for their animals, that there have been some serious clashes.

"The Bannock and Pitt River tribes have been horsemen for many generations, and they are very resentful of the white incursions. We will be riding into and through their country on this trail, but they rarely attack anything smaller than a group with many animals they can take."

"That's good to know," Chance smiled back. "I've heard of this Captain Sou you ride with. Quite a leader, eh?"

"Very good man, Marshal. Very good." He was looking down at the trail from time to time as he talked, and looking around at high mountains to their east, and lower mountains to the west. "Those mountains east," he said, gesturing toward them, "are what the white people call the Santa Rosa Mountains. The Paradise Valley, which we left just a few minutes ago, swings around to the northeast, and then parallels the mountains north. Very good hunting, and several white people have made ranches in the valley.

"We will come to a pass on the left in a few minutes, that if we took it, would lead us to the Queen's River, and down into the Black Rock Desert. I would think the man we are following would continue north, not take that trail."

"The man we're following has never been in this country, Mr. Cougar, so we might want to keep our eyes open, just in case. He is not trail-wise, and is not a horseman. He is a known killer, so we must be aware at all times."

"You may simply call me Cougar, if you like Marshal," he said, giving Chance just a slight smile. He sat tall on his horse, was obviously very strong, and sure of himself, but did not show signs of arrogance or ego. He had his long black hair tied back, wore buckskins under a heavy wool robe he kept tightly wrapped, and Chance could see tall moccasins on the man's feet.

Chance was wrapped just as tightly in his bearskin jacket as they continued on the trail at a fast trot. "I see your moccasins, Cougar, but how do you keep your feet warm? Mine are frozen right now."

"Good insulation," he said, again giving Chance that sly smile, as if he had just told a little joke. "We stuff grass inside the moccasins, then slip our feet in. My feet are comfortable right now, even in this bitter cold." Chance just shook his head, getting another slight smile from the big Indian.

Not having to break trail through crusted snow and ice, they were making good time at a solid trot as the day wore itself well into late afternoon. "We should find a fair place to camp in about fifteen miles," Cougar said, "with water and grass for the animals. It's off the trail some, so not too many people know about it."

"We need to watch for horse tracks that might indicate a tired or sore animal. Stokes is a fool when it comes to horses, and will ride a horse to its death. He has all but ruined two horses since I started this chase. He'll kill in a minute to get another if the one he stole gives out on him."

A bitter cold wind was blowing down from the north, and the clouds that were beginning to pile up told the two that they would be riding into the teeth of another winter snowstorm well before they reached the camp area. "If that horse gives out, he'll be looking to get another, and with this storm brewing, he'll be desperate."

They rode in silence for the next couple of hours, their eyes scouring the trail, trying to pick up something from the tracks. Cougar spoke up as they topped a small hill, pointing at the trail. "Looks like the only horse that's been through here in the last several hours is the one Stokes stole. See, here," and he pointed at a set of prints. "That horse is favoring his right front foot. He was riding hard and has slowed down, now." The two dismounted and looked closely at the track.

"I don't see any blood, so it might be a twisted joint, maybe a pulled muscle, maybe even a bruise from a rock or chunk of ice, but you're right, he's favoring that foot." Chance looked as far up the trail as he could see, but there was nothing to see. "Let's get back on it," he said, mounting Mr. Morgan and taking up the lead rope to the mule. "We'll be losing light before too much longer, and that storm is gonna smack us a good one tonight."

As the two made a turn around a rock outcropping, they saw two men walking alongside the trail, about half a mile ahead. "Something wrong," is all Cougar said, and they nudged their animals into a little faster trot. "Men don't go walking in this country."

"One of them is limping, Cougar," Chance shouted through the increasing wind. The two men heard their approach and stopped, waiting for them, waving their arms just in case they hadn't been seen.

"You boys have some trouble?" Chance asked, stepping off the big stud, making sure the two saw his badge. Cougar took the reins from the marshal, and the lead rope from the mule and did not dismount, just in case something bad happened.

"Some bastard rode up behind us, real fast, shot my partner, and stole our horses. He just turned the horse he was on loose and chased it off, and we couldn't catch it after he left."

"I'll get it," Cougar said, handing the leads and ropes to Chance. "You men are lucky to be alive." He rode off, seeing the still saddled horse munching on some grass a couple of hundred yards away.

"What are you men doing out here, anyway?" Chance asked, taking a look at the bullet wound to one of the men's leg. "Just chewed up some meat," he said. "You'll live."

"We ride for old man Swanson, just making a circle to bring some strays in before this storm hits. Ranch is on the other side of that mountain there." Cougar rode up with the lame horse and Chance took a look at the sore leg.

"Just a pulled muscle, I think. If you boys take it real slow, he'll get you back to the ranch, but I'd find a camp for tonight and let him rest and get some grass in him. Did that fool that stole your horses say anything?"

"He was snarling, almost like an animal, and rode off at a full gallop, screaming at the horses."

"You're very lucky to be alive," is all Chance said, and he and Cougar remounted and rode off at a trot, ever northward. The first flakes of snow began swirling in the wind, gathering to gale force. "Better find that campsite pretty soon, Cougar, or we won't be able to see, I'm afraid."

"About ten more minutes, Marshal."

***

The brunt of the massive storm smashed into northern Nevada, engulfing Jim Stokes in swirling snow and wind so cold the breath would freeze onto whiskers. He didn't let up, pushed the horses hard, never let them slow to catch their breath. After two hours of hard riding, the horse being trailed threw a fit, pulled loose from its bridle, and ran off, free from constraint. Stokes anger boiled over and he took two shots at the fleeing horse, not hitting it, but screaming obscenities.

Stokes calmed down a little, didn't even try to catch the horse, just kept riding hard. Within half an hour, the horse he was on quit on him, stopping in the middle of the trail, gasping for air, the icy wind searing its lungs. Stokes spurred the horse viciously, to no avail, and finally dismounted. "No good son of a bitch," he snarled, and gave thought to shooting the animal, catching himself just in time.

He spotted a stand of juniper and Piñon pines several hundred yards off the main road and walked the horse to them, simply tying the worn out animal to a tree limb. The horse was able to kick snow aside for grass, but was tied so tight, he couldn't reach down and get any. Stokes gathered some wood, and finally managed to get a fire started, despite the heavy snow and high wind. He had no food or provisions of any kind with him, and searched the saddlebags of the frustrated horse, still trying desperately to get some fresh grass.

"Stand still, damn it," Stokes snarled at the animal, taking the saddlebags back to the fire. He found some dried meat and a couple of hard biscuits in the bags, and discovered a small tin of coffee in the bottom, but nothing to brew it in. Anger boiled through the man and he flung the contents of the saddlebags into the fire, cursed at the top of his lungs, and walked to his horse, jerking the reins loose.

The horse immediately dropped its head and started munching grass, which made Stokes even angrier than he was. He jerked the reins and the horse, probably just as angry as Stokes, whirled and tried to kick him. Stokes raised a fist to strike back, and the horse kicked again, breaking Stokes' arm.

He howled in pain but did not let go of the reins, and as he settled down into the snow, the horse pawed away at a patch of grass and began eating. Stokes got back to his feet after a few minutes and led the horse back toward his fire, threw some wood on the flames, and let the horse find grass, but not letting go of the reins. The pain from the solid kick slowly changed to an ache that extended from his wrist to his shoulder, and as shock set in, he felt he might lose consciousness.

While he could, he threw more wood on the fire and tied the reins to the base of a juniper tree, close to the fire. The night was filled with agonizing pain and bitter cold. Twice he awoke to feed the fire and each time had to brush off several inches of snow. By sunrise, the wind had reached more than gale force, there was two feet of snow or more on the ground, with drifts caused by the wind that would be measured in yards. His horse was still tied to the juniper tree and was in far better shape than he was.

He built up the fire, found a limb that was fairly straight and tried to tie it to his broken arm, making him scream at the frightful pain. *I should have done this last night,* he thought, finally getting his neckerchief tied around the arm and limb. He was dizzy, probably from a lack of food and water and the effects of shock, but he managed to get his horse untied from the tree, and got mounted.

He rode back to the main road, desperate to get to the Jordan Valley, not even knowing where that was or how far it might be. He had no idea he was being followed, only knew he had to keep moving. *I should have killed those two cowboys and taken their money. I need food. My arm hurts.* He was delirious, in and out of consciousness, and angry at the damned horse.

The horse refused to move faster than a trot, so he spurred it viciously, and slapped it with the reins over and over. The dizziness continued through the morning hours and at one time Stokes caught himself falling out of the saddle. He wasn't aware that he had passed out. The horse was moving at a slow walk, and Stokes was holding on as tight as he could, pain from the broken arm coursing through his body, hunger and thirst adding to his problems.

His mind was so fouled with hate, pain, and anger that he wasn't aware that he could have melted snow for water, didn't bother to make coffee after finding it in the saddlebags, and managed to throw the hard biscuits into the fire. Another hour and Jim Stokes would be dead.

***

It was young Jack McNaughton, breaking through huge drifts of snow, looking for cattle caught in the blizzard, who found him. Stokes was slumped in the saddle, unconscious, his horse just standing, tail to the howling wind. McNaughton couldn't wake him up, and took the reins, and the cow pony responded, willing to follow.

McNaughton was several miles from the main ranch, had been out most of the day, gathering what he could of the herd. This was his final, short circle, and he had just three steers gathered when he found Stokes. It took a couple of hours to drive the cattle in.

He brought Stokes to the ranch where his father was bringing in the milk cow and getting ready for evening chores. "He's pretty bad hurt, Pa," Jack yelled through the howling wind, coming into the barn.

Jack and Samuel McNaughton eased Stokes out of the saddle and laid him out on a pile of straw. "Take care of that horse, Jack. Hey, wait," he was pointing at the brand. "Isn't that Henry Swanson's brand? This isn't Swanson's grazing land. What the hell's he doing here? Swanson'll hear about this," McNaughton stormed.

"Well, take care of the horse, Jack, and I'll see what I can do for this yokel, find out what the hell he thinks he's doing on my grass." He untied the limb from Stokes's arm and got his heavy coat off. "Busted that arm a good one, he did," the old man muttered. "Shame your ma died," he yelled at Jack. "She'd know how to fix this. You want to help me here? Let's get him in the house before he freezes to death."

McNaughton's spread was second only to the Swanson Ranch in that section of Nevada. The two men, father and son, worked a large cow-calf operation, seldom hiring anyone, unless they needed an extra hand for a short time. Big Sam is how the father was usually referred to, while son Jack was actually the larger of the two, some called him a giant. His strength matched his size.

They trailed their herd north to the mining areas in the Jordan Valley, and east into the Boise area, for slaughter. The market was good and building fast, with new immigrants coming in by the thousands. Jack McNaughton got the saddle off the horse, wondered why there wasn't a set of saddlebags, wondered too, why the rider wasn't dressed as a buckaroo. "That boy was looking for trouble, going out in this weather with no chaps, no working gloves, and no canteen," he said to his father.

Jack picked Stokes up as he would a small child and carried him into their modest ranch house where a blazing fire had the rooms nicely heated. "Just put him up in the loft, I guess," Big Sam said.

"He didn't have anything with him, Pa. No saddlebags, no bedroll, nothin'. Ain't never seen a buckaroo in this country ride out with nothin'."

"Ain't never seen Swanson's hired help ride alone, either," Big Sam said. "S'pose he coulda got himself lost, but that don't make no sense either. Well, don't matter, let's get the fool cleaned up and in that bed. When he's warm he'll come to and we'll get some answers. Like what he's doin' on our range.

"Swanson'll hear about this, Jack. He likes to expand his grazing area, and I'll be damned if he's gonna expand into ours. Did you see any sign of Swanson cattle out there today? Well, hell, how could you, with snow coming down like a curtain across a window."

"I was lucky to get the cattle I got, Dad," Jack answered. "This buckaroo is lucky I even was able to see him. This is the worst blizzard I think we've ever had around here. 'Bout as bad as the floods were."

Chapter Twelve

Chance and Cougar rode into a small grove of ancient cottonwood trees as the storm arrived in all its fury, driving snow and ice right through their coats and blankets. Cougar took charge of the animals and Chance did his best to gather firewood and get a camp of sorts set up.

It took some serious savvy to get the fire started with winds howling and snow blowing, but they did, huddled in bushes under the bare trees. "A man should be smart enough not be out in this weather," Chance joked, watching Cougar try to pour a cup of boiling coffee. They took turns nursing the fire during the night, had fits of sleep, and got an early start.

"Can't see anyone's tracks now, Marshal. This is one of those northers that piles snow as high as a tree and then freezes it in place." Cougar and Chance spent the morning burrowed behind some low cedar bushes, nursing some sickly flames, and couldn't tell whether it was sunrise or not when they moved back on the chase following a brief breakfast of coffee and biscuits.

"Glad you found these cottonwoods, Cougar," Chance said. "That would have been a killer without a fire last night. Can you estimate how far we might be from Fort McDermitt? Are there any ranches between here and the fort where Stokes might hole up?"

"Even our tracks are covered within minutes," Cougar muttered. "Best bet, I think is to continue to Fort McDermitt. If my senses are still working, it should be about twenty miles ahead."

Both men were bundled against a howling and freezing wind and blanketed in a covering of heavy snow. They walked their horses through drifts as high as four and five feet, not always sure they were even on the main road. "If that fool lived through whatever happened to him back there, and if he's still pushing that horse as hard as he has been, we'll find either Stokes or his horse dead. Or both," Chance spat through frozen lips.

"We should watch for lumps along the trail, might be a body under the snow. The way Stokes treats his horses, he could get throwed and die in this blizzard. Make my job easier." The men were conversing using the least amount of words, trying to keep the blistering cold from freezing their lips and faces.

"See those trees through the snow?" Cougar said, pointing at some shadows several yards off the trail. "Looks like smoke over there." They rode quickly and found where Stokes had spent the night. "This is one poor excuse for a rough camp," Cougar said, looking at the mess the boy left.

"Why would he try to burn the saddlebags?" Chance was sifting through the snow and coming up with few answers.

"I think he's hurt," Cougar said. "These limbs and chunks of wood aren't broken like a fit man would break them. He's got a wound that won't let him use both hands. Maybe that guy in Winnemucca did hit him when he shot."

"If he's hurt and out in this miserable weather, we should catch up to him soon," Chance said, as the two got back in the saddle. "If he's not hurt, he will be when we catch him. He's gone at least two days without food, maybe even more than that, and if he's hurt on top of that, we'll find him soon.

"You check me for frostbite from time to time and I'll check you. Wind and cold like this and we're in a heap of trouble, Cougar, if we start to freeze up. Trailed a man in Wyoming one time and got caught in a blizzard like this. I found an old line-shack and huddled for a day or two, melting snow for water.

"Found my man's body less than a hundred feet from that shack, but not until the following spring. I must have walked right across his body getting there and leaving, and never knew he was there. We might not find Stokes until spring if he continues acting as stupid as he has been."

Ice drooped from every nose, horse, mule, and man, and snow covered every inch of them all as they moved down the trail, not seeing anything but that gray/white wall of blowing and drifting snow. "It's hard to judge distance or direction when there's nothing to see, Marshal, but I'm pretty sure we're still on the main road."

Chance snickered at the comment and said, "That's certainly good to know," which brought a good-natured chuckle from Cougar as well.

The morning wore itself slowly into afternoon, which drifted endlessly into evening before they found the all-but-brand-new army post at the northern edge of Nevada. "I'm not sure how you managed to keep us on the trail, Cougar, but I'm sure glad you are along with me. We'll have to be a little careful for a few minutes, because if Stokes is here, he might come at us. These soldier boys won't know he's a wanted killer."

Cougar said he'd take care of the animals while Chance paid a visit to the post commander. He stepped off the big stud, handing the lead ropes to Cougar. "I am stiff and frozen, Cougar. It's actually hard to walk, I'm so cold." Cougar gave Chance a big smile and agreed with him completely.

"Somewhere soon, Chance, I'm going to find a wood stove and get as close as I can get." He watched Chance plow through deep snow toward the Post Commander's office.

"Captain Wells, it's a pleasure to meet you. I'm Jacob Chance, U.S. Marshal," Chance said through still half-frozen lips, slipping out of his heavy bearskin coat, revealing his badge of office.

"It's a pleasure, Marshal," the fort's commander said. "Looks like you could use some hot coffee. How about a touch of Kentucky to spruce it up a bit," and he poured the coffee, producing a flask from a desk drawer.

"Most grateful, Captain. I'm tracking a killer who was on the Jordan Valley road. This massive blizzard has wiped out his trail, but he was just hours from here when it hit. Has a young man on a worn out horse come to the fort, either yesterday or today?"

"The only visitors we've had are local Indians and a few ranchers and their cowboys getting away from the storm. There are three main ranches in this area, the McNaughton spread is probably the closest, a larger operation is Henry Swanson's, and then north, on the Oregon side of the border, is a ranch called the OYE.

"Your man could be at either McNaughton's or Swanson's. I doubt he would have bypassed the fort to get to the OYE." The post commander paused briefly, then continued. "This is rough country, and while most of the local Indians are friendly, we do have encounters with the Bannock and once in a while, those from the Pit River country. Men don't travel alone much in this country."

"Can you arrange quarters for me and my Paiute tracker Cougar, sir? We'll spend a day or two here, hope the storm lets up, and start our search at the ranches. May have to make McDermitt our headquarters."

Captain Wells called his orderly in and gave him orders to arrange housing for Chance and Cougar. "You're welcome to stay as long as it takes, Marshal. Tell me about this man you're after so I can alert my people."

Chance spent the next hour, and one full pot of coffee with Wells, telling about young Jim Stokes, finishing by saying, simply, "He's just a bad man, almost as if he was born to be bad. There's not an ounce of compassion in his body."

***

"Eyes like Cougar," a voice called out in the Paiute language, as the large Indian moved the horses across the parade grounds and toward the corrals. "What brings you so far north, my brother?" a man in buckskins and wrapped tightly in a wool blanket, spoke from the entrance to a barn and stables.

"Raven," Cougar called, immediately. "I don't have to see you to know you," and the two embraced, Raven ushering Cougar into the barn. "So, you too have found a home with the army. Are they good to you?"

"I keep the horses and mules, so if they aren't they don't enjoy the animals they end up with," and the two chuckled over the thought. "One man, though, Sergeant Cornelius Amster, says he hates Indians, and can be mean when he's drunk, which is often.

"Just like so many whites, he doesn't know the difference between a Paiute and a Comanche, and if one Indian did him wrong, or he heard about an Indian doing something wrong, then all Indians have done that."

"I, too, have seen that in some," Cougar responded, pulling saddles and packs from the animals. "Ignorance is the answer. Some whites are intelligent, some are ignorant, and it's the latter that are dangerous." With Raven's help, he led the two horses and mule into stalls and feed.

"I'm riding with a U.S. Marshal, tracking a killer, Raven. We think he's injured, pretty sure his horse is mistreated, and he should have come here. He's a young man, large, mean, and has a heart full of hate. Anyone like that come through here in the last day or two?"

"Most visitors end up here with their animals, and you're the only one in the last few days, except for the locals. These storms have come down, one tumbling over the other, so not many people on the road." They walked back to the front entrance to the barn, watching the snow swirl and dance through the fort. "I have coffee in here,"

Raven said, leading Cougar into a small office, furnished with a blazing potbelly stove.

The men slipped out of their blankets and coats, Cougar rubbing his hands as near to the stove as he dared get, glorying in its warmth. "We had such a feeble fire last night," he laughed, "with howling winds, pounding snow, and green wood. This is good, Raven, this is good."

Raven produced some smoked venison and fry bread, and the two spent the next few hours catching up on each other, filling their bellies, and keeping the stove popping. Chance arrived in time to enjoy a cup from the third pot of the day, and spent another hour listening to stories from the two Paiute brothers.

"Your mama must have had a handful when you two were growing up," he laughed as he and Cougar put their coats back on to walk to their quarters. "Captain Wells has us set up in adjoining quarters. Let's grab our saddlebags and the packs from the mule. I think we'll be here for a few days, unless this storm keeps us longer.

"Wells said we're to meet with a Sergeant Amster and he'll show us to our quarters. We'll have to make some rides to a couple of nearby ranches. Stokes may have found one of them. It doesn't appear he made it here, at least not yet."

Cougar tightened slightly at the mention of Sergeant Amster but either Chance didn't notice or decided not to say anything, and Cougar didn't say anything either.

***

"Papa," Jack McNaughton yelled from the loft bedroom, down to the kitchen where Samuel was frying some side meat and potatoes for their supper. "This man is coming around. You better get up here." Jack was standing back from the bed as Jim Stokes aimed the revolver at him. "Hurry, Papa, he's got a gun."

"Damn Swanson riders are all alike," McNaughton snarled, grabbing his fowling piece and heading for the ladder leading to the loft. "Is this how a Swanson rider thanks someone?" he growled at Stokes. "Put that gun down or die on the spot," he said, leveling the large bore, double-barreled shotgun at him.

"Bring you out of the very mouth of death and you threaten the man that saved your worthless butt. Put it down," and Stokes could see the man's finger tighten on the trigger. He slowly lowered the weapon, but never quite let go of it, glaring, first at young Jack, then at his father.

He noticed his arm neatly bandaged, recognized he was in a bed, covered in warm wool blankets, and in a warm house. "Must have passed out," is all he said, as the revolver settled into the blankets, but still in his grip.

"My boy will take that gun, stranger, and if you argue, you're dead." Big Sam McNaughton was not in a mood to be trifled with, particularly with a howling blizzard fouling his work schedule on the ranch, with a neighboring cowboy riding his range, and now that jackass pulling a gun on his son. "I ain't killed a man in more than a year, but I surely remember how. Now, let go that damn gun."

Fury swirled through Stokes, a rage that he could not control, and at the same time he knew he could not take out both these men. He would be dead if he tried, and that made him even angrier. His fingers slowly uncoiled from the handle of the weapon and McNaughton shoved the big long gun closer to Stokes' head. "Take your hand away from that gun, now," and he prodded Stokes with the barrel, glaring at him just as hard as Stokes was glaring back.

Big Sam nodded to Jack who stepped forward slowly and retrieved the weapon. "What the hell were you doing riding on my range? Henry Swanson know you're over here?"

"Who the hell's Henry Swanson?" Stokes growled back, his face clouded in anger, frustration, embarrassment, and pain. "Ain't never heard the name. Who are you?" he said, trying to get his broken arm settled somewhere that it didn't hurt.

"You were riding a Swanson horse, mister. You don't know Henry Swanson? About makes you out as a horse thief," Sam said. "Maybe I'll just shoot your skinny ass anyway," and he snickered, bringing the big gun back into position.

"No, Papa," Jack said. "Let's find out what his story is before we hang him." He was admiring the revolver, testing the action, aimed it at Stokes a couple of times, with a nice smile on his face. "I found a whole bunch of money and gold in a bag he had underneath his big coat when I put the horse up. This fool might have a good story to tell."

"That money's mine," Stokes howled, trying to sit up in bed, the heavy covers holding him down. "You keep your filthy hands off it. It's mine."

Big Sam McNaughton slammed Stokes across the side of the head with the barrel of the shotgun, putting him down for the count. "We'll bundle this foul mouthed critter off to the army fort soon's the damn weather allows. Hope we don't find out he killed old Henry and stole that money.

"Well, come on back down stairs for supper. No, wait. Get some rope and tie this asshole to the bed. He's one dangerous man, I think. Then, we'll eat and count that money you found. Always have enjoyed counting money," he chuckled, taking the ladder back down to the kitchen.

***

"Lookin' for Sergeant Amster," Chance said as they entered the wooden barracks. "I'm U.S. Marshal Jacob Chance and this is Cougar. Captain Wells said he has quarters set up for us."

The private stood up straight when the men entered, and a frown came across his face as Chance introduced himself. "The sergeant is over at the suttler's store, sir. I don't think you are allowed to bring an Indian into the BOQ, sir. Sergeant Amster sure wouldn't allow that."

"We'll see about that. Where are our quarters, and I mean right now." The private jumped at the tone of voice and led the two down a long hallway, indicating the two rooms, side-by-side, and opened the doors.

"Set us up, Cougar, and I'll go find this Amster feller. Where's this suttler's store?" he growled at the private, marching back toward the entrance. The soldier gave him directions and Chance stepped back out into the teeth of the blizzard.

"Sergeant Amster in here?" he asked, entering a filthy building that stunk like a garbage pit. Several men in uniform were standing at a makeshift bar with bottles of whiskey in front of them. The clerk didn't answer Chance, simply pointed at the group of men.

"One of you men Amster?" Chance asked, stepping toward them.

"I am," one of them snarled. "What do you want?"

"Name's Chance, Jacob Chance, U.S. Marshal. You were supposed to set up housing for my tracker and me. All I saw was an empty room with an unmade bed. I want those rooms set up and ready now, Sergeant."

"I don't take orders from civilians," Amster spit out, turning back to his bottle. Chance grabbed him by the shoulder and spun him around, pulled his revolver, and shoved it into the sergeant's face, lightly touching the end of the sergeant's nose.

"The captain gave you a direct order and I aim to see to it that it's carried out soldier. Do you want to walk back to the quarters or would you rather I drag you by your balls?" Chance shoved the barrel of the big gun right into one of Amster's nostrils.

The silence in the general store wasn't broken for almost thirty seconds as soldiers of various rank saw their leader slowly fold and give in, something that hadn't been seen before. Shuffling feet broke the silence as the men backed away from what looked like it could turn ugly in a blink of an eye.

Chance's eyes were narrowed, his mouth set, and the gun cocked, and Amster whispered, "All right, let's go," and Chance pulled the revolver down, didn't uncock it nor did he put it back in leather, and the two men walked out into the storm. "Ain't no foul Indian gonna sleep in the BOQ," Amster said. "He can sleep in the barn."

"He'll be sleeping in his own room at the BOQ, Sergeant. Captain Wells will hear about this insubordination. Cougar is working with a federal law enforcement officer and will be treated with the respect that demands. You had best understand that fully." Amster wasn't walking as fast as Chance wanted, and he prodded him some, giving him a little shove.

Amster spun around and planted a fist in the middle of Chance's face, sending the marshal sprawling in the snow. Amster jumped on him and Chance wrapped his long arms around the sergeant, spinning, and turning him over on his back. He led with a left, followed with a right, and drove another left down into the sergeant's face, smashing his nose flat.

Chance jumped to his feet, pulled Amster to his feet, and pasted him twice more with straight-from-the-shoulder jabs, knocking the man down. Chance retrieved his revolver from the snow, where it fell when the sergeant pasted him. "You just committed one serious crime, Sergeant. You attacked a federal marshal, and the man I'm chasing did the same thing a couple of years ago. I let that man off, but I'll be damned if I'll let you off. The Captain will have you in irons if I have anything to say about it.

Now, get up off your skinny butt and get my quarters set up."

Amster was slow to get up and Chance was about to hit him again when the sergeant held up his hand in defeat. "No more," he whimpered, and Chance spun him around and pushed him toward the barracks.

"See to it these men's rooms are set up properly, Private, with clean bedding and wood for the stoves."

"Thank you, Sergeant," Chance said, smiling, nodding to the private. "Where's the mess and what time is supper served?" he asked, overly polite.

"Colors at five, supper is served at six," the private answered, staring at the battered face of his sergeant, desperately wanting to know the story behind the blood, knowing he could not even think about asking. "I'll have your rooms ready as soon as I can," he said, and scurried down the long hallway.

Chance clapped Cougar on the shoulder and the two walked out into the storm, heading for the post barns. "Let's take care of our animals, shall we?" he smiled, giving his tracker a wink as well. "They could use a good rubdown and some oats, if there are any."

"You don't look like a Paiute, Marshal. You wouldn't lie to me about being a white man, would you?" and Cougar was laughing all the way to the barns, and spent the first ten minutes telling Raven the story when they got there. "Fists like iron," Cougar said. "U.S. Marshal Fists Like Iron is the man I'm working with right now."

The merriment continued until after colors, and Chance and Cougar walked to Post Headquarters and joined Captain Wells for supper. "Rumors spread fast in a small environment like our post, Marshal. What exactly happened between you and Sergeant Amster?"

Chance spared no detail telling the story and made it clear that the sergeant should be brought up on charges. "Army post or not, enlisted man or not, he aggressively knocked me on my butt," Chance smiled, "and if you don't charge him, I will. I am a federal law enforcement officer and I can't let this be ignored."

"I'll see to it, Marshal. Have you made any plans for finding the outlaw?"

"Everything will be determined by this blizzard, I'm afraid. I know for a fact we haven't lost him, but it may take some doing to find him. Even when the storm lets up, nobody will be moving anywhere fast, and that includes us."

The storm howled for the entire next day, snow drifting into great mounds, forcing the post soldiers to almost dig tunnels between the buildings, and on the morning of the third day, the men could see breaks in the clouds, actual sunlight poured down, blindingly white, surrounded by blue skies.

"Time for us to get back to work, Cougar," Chance said as the men enjoyed a hot breakfast of oatmeal and coffee. "Captain Wells tells me it's about ten miles to the McNaughton Ranch, and with theses drifts, it might take us most of the day to get there. We need to bring the mule and a pack."

"That other ranch, the Swanson spread," Cougar said, "was where those two cowboys were from. It's some distance from here, on the east side of those mountains. Stokes was heading away from that area, Chance."

"We'll concentrate on the main road from here and then to McNaughton's. We must have ridden right by the road to McNaughton's the other day and not even seen it." Chance was brushing his big stud, contemplating what Cougar had said. "I'm sure that fool didn't ride right on past the fort here, but I'm not sure we would have seen him if he fell off his horse. If we don't find him frozen along the trail, we'll find him at the McNaughton Ranch."

Chapter Thirteen

"I been shoveling for two hours, Papa," Jack McNaughton complained, "and I still can't get the barn doors open. I've never seen this much snow." Big Sam McNaughton wanted to get the wagon out of the barn and hitched to a team so they could make the long ride to Fort McDermitt. The snow had drifted as high as eight feet across the front of the barn, coming in great swirls, demons shrouded in white, Big Sam said once. "I can't even see the corral fences. Even if we put the sleigh runners on that wagon, I doubt the horses can plow their way through these drifts."

"Do the best you can, Jack. Maybe the sunshine will help clear some of this out. We may be better off just tying that miserable outlaw to a saddle horse, and us riding to the fort. Still need to get them doors open."

Big Sam had never been known for having patience, was quick to anger and just as quick to calm back down, but for three days he had been stuck in the house, and with the outlaw moaning and complaining, Sam was ready to do something, anything, to get away from him. "I'll tell you now, Jack, we either get them horses out of the barn and saddled or I'm gonna take that fool by the neck and tie him to a tree and let him rot."

"Take it easy Papa. Throw some wood on the fire, rough that bad man up some, you've been craving that for a few days, and make him ready for the ride. I'll get the horses and things ready." He was smiling as he left the warm kitchen for one more trek to the barn. *He loves to talk like this big old mean man, and it works on some people, but I know him too well,* Jack was smiling making his way through the drifts.

For the last three days Jack had been using an outside ladder to access the barn through the hayloft, to feed the animals and milk the old cow, all trapped inside. He spent another hour with a shovel and was able to get one of the large doors open enough to move horses in and out. *Between the big floods last year and the blizzards this year, I better not hear Papa complain about water.* He made his way back to the house, planning on what to take for the ride to Fort McDermitt, and how to secure the outlaw to a horse.

Jim Stokes was still tied to his bed, only let partially loose to eat, and even then, one of the McNaughton's would stand close with the shotgun. During these past few days, Stokes' anger had risen to the point that Jack and Sam would dearly love to just shove him out the door and left him freeze to death.

"The flames of hell boil that man's blood, so's he probably would melt the ice instead of freezing," Sam growled, making Jack laugh right out loud. "Ought to just shoot the fool, freeze him up some, and take him to the fort come spring," Sam continued, but had to laugh right along with his son.

"Ma wouldn't like that talk, Papa," Jack chuckled, pouring them cups of boiling coffee. "What do you suppose it is that makes a man as angry and mean as him? He would have shot me the other day, and all we done is fix his arm, get him warm, and feed him. Ain't that what the book says we should do?"

"Yeah, it is, son, and your ma would be proud that we did it, but there ain't no accounting for the way some people react to kindness. Give me a week with that boy and he'd either be dead or he'd be calling me sir, and with a smile on his face."

"You like to think you're so tough and mean, Papa, but you ain't never laid a hand on me, and mama always called you a cute little kitten," Jack was chuckling, watching Big Sam squirm some, and frown, and then break into a big smile.

"I'm gonna whack you one day, boy, you just wait and see," and he feigned a punch, Jack dodging out of the way with ease. "You're right though. That boy's alive because of you, and instead of giving thanks, he's wantin' to kill you. Ain't right the way some people are. I'd be on bended knee tellin' you what a fine man you was, helpin' to save my life.

"Well, let's bring that fool downstairs here, tied up good and tight, and get ready to head to the fort. I'd prefer the wagon but I guess with what we're looking at out there, we better go saddle back."

"I'm gonna pack extra blankets and food, Papa. It might get nasty out there, and we ain't gonna get any help from that outlaw. Just some hard biscuits and smoked meat, maybe coffee. Won't have much trouble getting water," he smiled, heading for the ladder to the loft.

"All right, fool, you're goin' for a horseback ride and if you make a move on me or my pa, I'm gonna shove a big ol' knife through your gut," and Jack whopped Stokes across the side of the head and got him on his feet. "Don't trip goin' down that ladder, boy," Jack snarled, feigning a push, watching Stokes' eyes light up with a touch of fear.

***

Raven helped Cougar and Chance get their horses saddled and the mule packed. The sun was shining, snow and ice were melting, and soldiers were mucking out pathways throughout the fort. "You watch those drifts," Raven said, slipping some smoked venison into Cougar's saddlebag. "Looks like you could get in trouble walking into a ravine that can't be seen."

"It'll take us a couple of days to make McNaughton's," Cougar said, "and we aren't in any big hurry. If Stokes is there, he won't be going anywhere. Take care, brother."

As Chance stepped into the saddle, Sergeant Amster appeared from behind the barn with a rifle in hand, brought it up and fired, knocking Chance right out of the saddle, a bullet through his upper left arm. Before the sergeant could get a second shot off, Raven leaped on the man and drove a long, heavy knife through his heart, standing up to watch the man bleed to death.

Cougar was off his horse and beside Chance in a flash, finding the marshal bleeding heavy, but fully conscious. "Let's get that bleeding stopped, Marshal," the big Paiute said, taking the marshal's neckerchief and wrapping it tightly around the wound. "No riding today, boss," he said, helping Chance to his feet.

The fort responded to the gunshot, soldiers dashing about, officers trying to determine what had happened, and finally, Captain Wells coming to the scene. "What the hell is going on?" he said, seeing Sergeant Amster's body, Raven with a bloody knife, and Marshal Chance holding his arm, still dripping blood.

It took less than a minute for Chance to tell the post commander what took place, going out of his way to thank Raven for saving his life. "We talked about your altercation with Amster last night," Wells said. "He was a hot-head. Lieutenant Smith, get a detail together and let's get Amster buried, Raven, take Marshal Chance to the post doctor, and the rest of you, continue cleaning up from the storm."

"If you had put that man under arrest, as I demanded last night, Captain Wells, this would not have happened. You have a dead trooper on your hands because you failed to take action. Now, I'm delayed in tracking down a murderer, and if I lose him because of this, your superiors will know about it in quick time."

The flash of anger was over in moments, and Chance turned to his partner. "Cougar, take care of the animals until I get back," he said as Raven led the way to the post medical facility. "That was very brave, Raven. Thank you, again."

"You don't know how long I've waited for that opportunity, Marshal Chance. My heart sings right now, and many Paiute in this neighborhood will sing as well. Many young girls will sleep better, many men will nod their heads in agreement with what happened."

"You're an eloquent man, Raven," Chance said as the two walked into the doctor's facility. "Head on back to the barn, I'll be fine, and I'm sure Cougar will have many things to say to you."

"It was my pleasure, Fists Like Iron," he said, chuckling, as he headed out the door. "My pleasure."

Fists Like Iron, he thought. *I'll have some fun with Jennifer when I get home. Sure wish I was there right now instead of chasing Stokes all over the damn state. This is my last ride, Jenny. I promise. At least all this is happening in the middle of winter and not taking away from my work on the ranch.*

He found himself contemplating life on the ranch often, thinking about Little Jake in relation to what he knows had happened with Jim Stokes. *Ben had to have some of these same thoughts while Jim and Jenny were growing up. I want Little Jake to be a man, a real man, not a damn criminal, but what will I have to do to make that happen?* If Jennifer had been there, she would have told him to just be Jacob Chance and let the boy see what a real man is like.

The doctor spent a couple of hours working on Chance's arm, finally getting the bullet out and the wound closed and dressed. "In relation to your body, if your arm hadn't been in the way, you'd be a dead man, Marshal Chance. As it is, your arm is going to hurt like a son of a bitch for some time. Try to keep the wound clean, redress it regularly, take a hefty shot of Kentucky for the pain."

"Best advice I've had," Chance laughed despite the pain. He snatched up the bullet, put it in his pocket, "Got a couple of these at home," he said, and got dressed. Some of the soldiers seemed to give him friendly looks, but others glared as he made his way to the post commander's office.

"Captain, I need some paper and pen, to write you a full report on what has happened. I'll need you to forward that report to Major Randall in San Francisco, and of course, to your superiors. I do not want to hear about repercussions aimed at Raven, and I'll not tolerate any coming in my direction."

"Neither will I, Marshal Chance. There are other hotheads on this post, others that simply hate any and all Indians, but my corps of officers will control them. I assume your plans have changed?" He did not attempt to apologize for not putting Amster in irons, nor did he mention the subject.

"Postponed, Captain, not changed. I'll give this wound a day or two, then Cougar and I will be back on the trail. It's important that your people understand that Stokes could still show up here, and understand that he kills without thought. I will expect you to place him under arrest if he does show up."

There was an implied threat in the statement and Chance's anger at the Captain was palpable, and every movement of his arm increased the anger by way of stabs of pain. *One man needlessly dead and me with a serious wound and all because this man failed in his duty. Not the man I initially thought he was.*

Chance spent an hour or two on his report to Captain Wells and Major Randall, and made his way across the parade grounds to the barn. "I brought a map from Captain Wells' office, Cougar, and we can figure out how we'll conduct our search. Let's plan on pulling out tomorrow morning, barring any more problems."

"Raven has ridden this country most of his life, Marshal, and has given me some good thoughts on where a fugitive might be able to hide out. You going to be well enough to ride by tomorrow?"

"Probably could right now, but the doctor said I have to take some medicine for the pain, and that's available at the suttler's store." He had a little-boy grin on his face, and it was Raven got the joke first, nudging Cougar into finally understanding.

Chance wasn't sure what kind of situation he might walk into at the store, and held his rifle lightly, ready to swing it into action at the slightest threat. Instead, he found several troopers simply moving aside as he stood up to the bar.

"Whisky," he said to the barkeep. "You gentlemen join me?" he asked.

"Yes, Sir," one piped up, with a smile. "It wasn't right for Sergeant Amster to shoot you, Marshal. He was drunk, and just acting stupid. Your arm gonna be okay?"

"Just fine, son, just fine." He spent about an hour with the troopers, had enough "pain medicine" to take its necessary effect, and made his way back to quarters and a good sleep.

***

"Ain't never seen drifts this deep," Big Sam McNaughton was riding his best cow pony, leading Jim Stokes, trussed tightly, and then Jack McNaughton trailing a well-packed mule. He and Sam traded off leading every hour or so, so the horses didn't tire-out from busting through snow as much as five feet or more in places.

Stokes fought like an army mule when the McNaughton's tied him into the saddle, screaming in pain when his broken arm was twisted or wrenched, more from his own movements than from anything either Sam or Jack did. "Shut your stupid mouth, boy," Big Sam said more than once, whacking him across the side of the head.

"I think you were right, Jack. Just shoot the bastard, let him freeze and bring the filthy body to the army come spring."

"Still have time to do that, Papa," Jack smiled back, fingering his old, almost worn out, cap and ball musket. "Deerslayer," that's what Jack jokingly called his muzzle loader, "is primed and I got a cap in place." After three days of listening to Stokes rant, complain, and scream obscenities, either man would willingly pull the trigger.

"Caught in a blizzard with a broken arm, no food, no water, no way to light a fire, and only a stupid man would act this way," Sam said, jerking the ropes as tight as possible, pleased with the resulting howl of pain. "You should have eaten your breakfast, fool, cuz we ain't stoppin' 'till it's either dark or we're at Fort McDermitt. Saddle up, Jack, and let's move."

The miles crept by, the lead horse tiring quickly from breaking trail. It was during a switch, when Sam stopped and waited for Jack to move up to take the lead that Stokes performed one more stupid stunt. Jack was handing off the lead rope for the mule when Stokes jammed his spurs into the ribs of his horse.

The well-trained Swanson Ranch cow pony leapt forward and tried to race away, Stokes heehawing and spurring the animal on. Jack McNaughton spent hours every spring and fall moving hundreds of cows and calves, most that didn't want to be moved, and he and his horse worked as a single unit.

Spinning quickly, taking three long leaps, Jack was alongside Stokes, rifle raised, and he slammed it down on the outlaw's skull, knocking him right out of the saddle. Jack was off his horse in a flash, and jammed the barrel of the rifle into Stokes's chest. "What's the word, Papa?" he said, looking up at Big Sam.

Stokes was unconscious, bleeding heavily, and Sam McNaughton shook his head. "Man's a lunatic, Jack. Can't shoot crazy people. Let's get him back on that horse." It took some doing in heavy wet snow to get Stokes in the saddle after first wrapping his head in some rags to stop the bleeding.

"You whupped him a good one, Jack. Won't be listening to his foul mouth for the rest of this trip, I'm thinkin'." Stokes was slumped in the saddle, tied tightly to the saddle this time. "Doubt if a man could live through a whuppin' like that," he murmured, climbing back on his horse. "You lead for awhile, Jack. I've got the mule."

Sunshine falling on the drifted snow allowed the surface to melt just a little bit, and as the day wore on and evening shadows crept across the landscape, the melt turned to ice, making busting trail that much more difficult. "I'm trying to figure out how far we've come, Papa. Been on the trail for hours but I don't think we've made much distance."

"Got some cottonwoods coming up on our right, Jack, and that should be Mary's Bend. Let's make camp there, and we'll be about five long miles from the fort in the morning. These animals are worn out and trying to go on in the dark will just make it worse, I'm afraid.

"That boy hasn't woke up, and I ain't checked. Might be dead already."

Jack led the group to the trees and camp was made with difficulty, trying to clear snow, find some dry wood, and get Stokes laid-out near the fire. "He didn't die but he sure as hell ain't breathing right, Papa," Jack said, adding some large limbs that had broken off one of the trees to the fire.

"Just doesn't feel right, Papa. Here it is, I saved this man's life, we nursed him and fed him, and now, I may be the man that killed him. Just doesn't feel right, somehow."

He and Sam got Stokes laid out and in a blanket as close to the fire as they dared.

"Glad I packed this food and coffee," the young man said, setting the pot on a rock next to the fire.

"I'm glad I brought this," Big Sam said, getting a flask from his heavy coat. "This always makes the coffee better."

"If that man dies, will I be in trouble, Papa?" Jack asked, nursing his coffee with some sweetener from the flask as well. "Will they think I murdered him?"

"I won't let that happen, Jack. I don't want the boy to die anymore than you do, but he is an outlaw, and I'm sure someone is looking for him. We know he had to steal that Swanson horse, and God knows where all that money came from." He took a long drink from the tin cup and filled it back up with coffee.

"No, you won't be charged with anything as long as I'm alive. You should be given the reward, if there is one. You did the right thing, boy, and your ma would be proud."

Chapter Fourteen

Sunrise found Chance and Cougar saddled, packed, and on the road to the McNaughton Ranch, some twenty miles distant. "Snow's crusted bad," Cougar said when they moved onto the main road. "This will be a slow ride, Chance. That ice could tear up the horses' legs and put us on the ground."

"We'll go as slow as it takes, Cougar." With Raven's help they had wrapped the front feet of all three animals in heavy buckskin and wool, and they walked single file, planning on changing leads every hour or so. "If Stokes is at one of the ranches, we'll find him, and he can't go any faster than we can, if he tries to run some more. He stole a ranch horse, and they just won't put up with being mistreated."

They rode slow, breaking through a crust of ice on top of the snow that in some places had drifted as high as five feet. It was an incredibly beautiful morning, a bright winter sun shining through a deep blue sky, and Chance was thinking, *no wind.* The main road meandered through the northern Nevada landscape offering glimpses of mule deer taking advantage of grass under cottonwood trees, ravens dancing their own brand of ballet in the thin, cold air, and towering mountains cloaked in next summer's water.

They roused a bunch of antelope napping under heavy sage brush, scattering the herd through the deep drifts. "Look at them run," Chance said. "Looks like they're dancing across the ice crust, not even breaking through.

"Looking around us, it's hard to realize we're tracking a man who has murdered several people, stolen horses, and destroyed other people's lives. I retired once from doing this job, and when I catch this fool, I will retire again, and for good." Chance was talking as much to himself as to Cougar, who at the time was in the lead.

"Better hunting and fishing in the summer, Marshal Chance," Cougar said, looking back over his shoulder, "but this earth of ours is never more charming than mid-winter. We may not be praising all this tonight, though," he smiled, "when the temperature falls to below zero." Chance just harrumphed some, but did smile at the comment.

An hour and a half into the morning, they turned off the main road, heading east toward some high mountains in the distance. "According to Captain Wells, the McNaughton place is at the foot of those mountains and Swanson's is on the other side of the mountains." Chance was pointing at a distant ridge. "Is that what you called the Santa Rosa range?" he asked Cougar, getting a nod back.

"It looks like we'll have to camp out here tonight. I don't think we can make that much distance through this snow and ice. We'll ride into late afternoon and find some trees to camp under. We'll sure want a fire," he said, getting a vigorous nod back from his Indian partner.

"It's easy to see how we missed that turnoff the other day. We almost missed it today and there is no storm." Chance was talking more than usual, about things that had no direct meaning to their ride.

"Your arm hurts pretty bad, eh?" Cougar asked. "Talking does take your mind off the pain a little bit. Anytime you want to stop, just say so." He got a grunt back from the marshal, but it included a thank you smile.

The scenery was difficult to look at, blinding sunlight pouring down on snow that in some places was a deep blue, in others so white you couldn't look at it. Mountains were covered with trees bending from the weight of the snow, and the two caught glimpses of wild game trying to forage, and once in a while, a steer or heifer floundering about, looking for grass.

They kicked up sage grouse and quail often as they rode near a stand of trees or through heavy sagebrush. Large white hares would bound through the snow, and more than once they spotted single coyotes moving furtively about. "A hare that size," Cougar said at one sighting, "might fight off a coyote," and both men chuckled at the thought.

"Keep your eyes open for a good spot to make camp, Cougar. It would be best if it is somewhere close to the half way point, but let's keep the animals safe. A man on foot in this country would be a dead man."

***

"He's still breathin' funny, Papa, and he ain't gonna wake up. He quit bleedin' anyway," Jack McNaughton said, trying to get some response from Stokes. "I guess we'll just have to tie him back on that horse when we leave."

"Or just leave," Big Sam snarled. "I'm cold, didn't sleep a bit, I'm hungry, and all because you tried to help a stranger. Maybe we'll just dig a hole in the snow and leave the fool. Somebody'll find what's left come spring."

"Aw, Papa," Jack smiled, listening to the growling. "Let me get some coffee in you, and I'll fry up some of this venison I tucked in my pack, and you'll know we're doing the right thing, but you're right, it's because I tried to help a stranger." He got the fire roaring, had coffee boiling in minutes, and the smell of frying meat perked Big Sam up right away.

"I ain't gonna change, though," Jack said, pouring large tin cups full of the hot coffee. "I did the right thing bringing that fool in to help him. We're not wrong, Papa. He's wrong."

"You're right and I know it," Sam said, kneeling down as close to the fire as he dared, warming his hands and face. "Your Ma would be proud of you, and I think you know how I feel. If that fool had been a Swanson hand and we took him in and treated him right, old Henry would have said a friendly thank you, and this outlaw wanted to shoot you.

"Some people just ain't no good, Jack," he said, a sad look on his face. "Just ain't no good."

It was well after sunrise when they finally broke camp and were back on the trail to Fort McDermitt. "That sunshine yesterday melted the surface of the snow and we got ourselves a long slow ride, Jack. That ice crust will wreck these horses if we try to make a good ride."

"Ain't in no hurry, anyway, Papa. Think we can make it all the way today? That sun is really bright."

They were in the middle of trading lead when Jack spotted movement a mile or so up the trail. "Look, Papa," he said, and pointed out the dark spots moving on the trail. "Sure looks like three horses up there, and they be comin' our way."

"Damn," Big Sam spat. "If those are friends of this horse thief, we're in trouble. And if they're Swanson cowboys, sure as hell they'll blame us for having one of their horses." Sam loosened the belt holding his heavy coat closed and made sure his sidearm was loaded and ready for use.

"Check your weapons, Jack. Let's not take any stupid chances. This whole damn affair is stupid from start to finish. We should be back at the ranch taking care of things, not nurse maiding some fool outlaw."

Jack listened with a wry smile as he checked his revolver. "Don't be shootin' these guys comin' toward us just cuz you're upset," he said as he pulled that monster shotgun and checked its load. He stood tall in the stirrups shading his eyes to get a better look at the three horses coming up the trail.

"Man could go snow-blind in a hurry, on a day like this," Big Sam said. "Keep your eyes kinda half open, Jack. They ain't nothin' but snow, every where you look."

"Looks like two riders trailing a pack animal. Might be coming from the fort to check on us, Papa. They done that during the big flood last year," he said. "Remember?" Jack still got chills thinking about those massive thunderstorms that blasted in from the south. Three days of torrential rains had every ditch, creek, and depression running like the Mississippi, tearing out fences, ripping building right off their foundations, and drowning cattle, sheep, and horses.

"Yeah, I remember. I hope you're right, but keep your weapons ready, just in case." They had Stokes' horse and the pack mule behind them and sat their horses in the middle of the trail, watching the riders slowly come toward them. "They ain't army," Sam said, as they got closer.

"One's an Indian," Jack said, "and the other looks like a drifter or somethin'. Wearing a heavy coat and a sombrero. I'm gonna keep the shotgun in my hands when they get closer."

"Yeah, Jack, and don't be afraid of using it. Damn that stupid fool for finding us. I don't like any of this, and I might just shoot somebody just cuz I'm that way."

Jack had to chuckle, listening to Big Sam. "You talk such a mean streak, Papa, and every time, I remember Mama telling you to behave, and laughing while she said it. If you do shoot someone, make sure it's the bad guy, okay?" he laughed, watching the riders move closer.

When the two groups were about twenty-five feet apart, Big Sam McNaughton put his hand up. "That's far enough," he bellowed. "Who are you and what do you want?" Jack sat quiet cradling that scattergun and Sam had his hand wrapped around the handle of his revolver. "We got an injured man and we don't want any trouble. Don't offer any."

"Not giving trouble today," Chance smiled. "I'm Jacob Chance, U.S. Marshal and this is Eyes Like Cougar, my tracker. We've been trailing a bank-robbing killer named Jim Stokes. Is that him across the saddle?"

"Maybe," Jack McNaughton said. "I found him a few days ago with a broken arm riding a horse belonging to the Swanson Ranch. He's been more than a cantankerous fool ever since.

"I had to smash him across the head with this old scattergun yesterday. He's still out."

Chance nudged Mr. Morgan and rode up close to Stokes, all slumped but tied tight to the ranch horse. "This is Stokes," he said. "You must have hit him pretty hard," Chance said, "for him to still be unconscious."

"Tried to kill my Papa," is all Jack said. "Back at the ranch, he tried to kill me, too. I ain't got no nice things to say about the man. We tried to help him and he turned on us like a badger on a snake. Don't necessarily want the fool to die, but I didn't mind hurting him at all."

"He's killed at least three men," Chance said, shaking hands with Jack and Sam. "You did right in protecting your father." He looked around at the trail, at Sam and Cougar, scratching the stubble of beard on his chin. "Looks like we're about half way between the fort and your ranch, McNaughton. Whichever way we go, Cougar, we're going to spend one more night in a snow camp."

"Me and Jack really want to get back to the ranch, Marshal. That outlaw has messed us up for too many days already, and with that storm that blew through, we got a mess back there." He was pleading and Chance knew what kind of problems a storm like this would cause to a cattle ranch.

"I can't say for sure, but it is possible that a reward has been offered for capturing this fool. If there has been, I'll see to it that you get it. You and Jack go on back to your ranch and Cougar and I will take Stokes back to Fort McDermitt."

"Thank you, Marshal," Jack said. "Will you ask the Army to see to it that the Swanson horse gets returned? Much obliged."

Everybody shook hands, all the way around, and Cougar took the lead rope for Stokes' horse, Chance had the lead rope for the pack mule, and they headed back toward the fort. Big Sam and Jack sat and watched for a few minutes, and turned back toward their ranch.

"Well, we know where a good camp site is for tonight, eh Jack?" Sam laughed, nudging his horse forward. "I want that fire so big they'll think the forest is burning like the embers from hell." He turned his horse to backtrack, and smiled a little bit. "Reward, eh? That sits well with me right now."

"Do you think I should have said something about all that money we found?" Jack asked. "That man probably stole it from someone."

"It appears to me that if he stole it, that marshal didn't know it, or he would have said something. Nope, that money is ours, payment for taking care of the fool and puttin' up with his nonsense. Besides, I want to count it again, just to make sure how much there is," and the two were still snickering when they rode back into the camp they had left hours before.

**

"We'll make a little better time going back," Cougar said, "with the trail broken by us earlier, but I don't think we will make it all the way. These horses are already pretty tired."

"We forded a little creek back there, near those big cottonwood trees, so let's pull up there for tonight. Probably about an hour or so away, I think. From the looks of things, we're only about a couple of hours from sunset anyway. That'll give us a good start in the morning."

The sun was getting low in the sky and the cold of evening hung heavy in the air as they pulled into a little cottonwood grove near the now frozen creek. "It'll be way below zero tonight," Chance muttered, undressing his Morgan stud and setting the hobbles. "At least there's enough downed wood to keep a good fire going. I'm worried about that boy, though. He shouldn't still be unconscious, even though he did take a pretty good lick."

The word concussion kept coming into Chance's head, and he knew that often led to eventual death. "I really want that boy to face Judge Stanfield, but that might not happen."

Cougar got a big fire going, the animals were well taken care of, and Stokes was laid out in a blanket near the fire. It didn't take long for boiling coffee to fill tin cups, with just a touch of Kentucky to 'smooth the bumps,' as Chance put it, and night was on them. "Glad we're prepared, Cougar. This wouldn't be a good night to go hungry."

Cougar sat very still, his eyes on a large sagebrush near the creek. Slowly he pulled his revolver, and using two hands, aimed and squeezed the trigger. "Hope you like rabbit, Marshal, but of course, if you don't, that would mean more for me," he chuckled, bringing back a large arctic hare with half its head blown away.

"How did you see that white rabbit in all this snow?" Chance asked, admiring the animal as Cougar quickly skinned and dressed it.

"I'm an Indian," is all the big man said, snorting some through a wide smile. The rabbit was skewered and slowly turned over the fire. "You won't find Paiutes going hungry in the winter."

"I've been wanting to ask you about something," Chance said, watching the rabbit roast. "That boy over there had the world handed to him by a loving father. He had a good life, raised on a large ranch, wanting nothing. He wasn't mistreated in any way, and had no personal responsibility, no sense of right and wrong, no compassion for anyone or anything.

"I'm married to his sister, and we have a son that we intend to raise with immense amounts of love and introduction to the ideas of personal responsibility, compassion, and understanding right from wrong.

"How were you raised? How do Paiute children become outstanding citizens, such as you are?"

"The old women mostly dictate how children are raised, and they are the ones to discipline, nurse, and teach the right ways. At a certain age, boys start learning the way men live, and girls, how women live. Children are seldom beat or whipped, but the learning can get a little rough sometimes," Cougar said, smiling broadly.

"It's not being allowed certain things that have the best results. Not being allowed to learn how to make a fine bow or straight arrows because of bad behavior has more effect on a Paiute boy than any whipping could have. Not being allowed to go on a hunt, or forced to stay behind while others take a long journey.

"I think it's all part of learning our history, being one with our world, understanding, as a child, what will be expected of us, and the fear of some things being denied. Some, like your man there, don't always make it."

Chance stirred the fire, added some wood, and they continued the conversation as they wolfed down a large arctic hare. "I just want my boy to be a real man when he grows up," Chance said. "Poor old Ben Stokes is heartbroken because of how Jim turned out. It was sad to watch," he said, throwing bones into the fire.

"Sure the best meal I've had in a long time," Chance said. "No salt, no vegetables, no pie, just one big fat hare roasted over an open fire. I could do this on a regular schedule, minus the below zero temperatures and icy cold bedroll I'm about to slip into."

Cougar smiled, threw the last leg bone from the rabbit into the fire, and pulled his blanket up tight. "Good night Fists Like Iron."

***

The sky was starting to come alive when Chance climbed out of his bedroll and threw large chucks of wood on the embers, getting a hot blaze going to ward off bitter cold. He filled the coffee pot with fresh snow, got that boiling and added coffee before Cougar finally rolled out. "You were snoring like a baby, Cougar. And, just so you know, I too saw two big rabbits this morning."

Chance knelt down at Stokes's side and eased the blankets back, seeing the ashen face of a dead man. "He didn't make the night," is all he said, settling down near the fire, coffee in hand. "I'm going to have to tell his father, and worse, my wife, his sister," he whispered, taking a platter of smoked venison from Cougar. "He had every opportunity any man could ever wish for a good life, now cut short.

"He had a ranch, a herd, a loving family, and a chance for a respectable life, and threw it away, became a killer and bank robber, a horse thief, with no compassion or thought for anyone but himself. Why?" Chance felt like he had done something wrong, let the boy down, or maybe let old Ben Stokes down.

"That boy didn't have to die this way, Cougar. He should be back in Preston, sitting on the porch of the Stokes' ranch house, telling whoppers with Ben and Jerrod Stockton and Cotton Phelps, not all stove up, broken bones and bashed in head, wrapped in frozen blankets, dead.

"When I get home I'm going to hold Jennifer so tight she'll think her ribs are breaking and I'm going to raise Little Jake to be the man that Jim should have been."

He looked into the eyes of Cougar, shaking his head in sorrow. "What a good life he could have had."

The ride was long and slow, fresh ice crusting over the trail they had broken the day before. It was late in the day when they rode through the gates of Fort McDermitt, Stokes' body draped across the saddle. They rode straight for the barns, greeted by Raven. Within minutes Captain Wells was on the scene.

"I'm going to need to write another report, Captain. Please see to it that he gets a decent burial. The grief that he has brought will be felt the length of this state. I will be leaving at dawn, and I want to tell you how much I appreciate your warmth and generosity to Cougar and me. I'll see to it your commander is aware of that."

"Thank you, Marshal. You will always be welcome at Fort McDermitt."

All the animosity of just three days before evaporated as Chance and Cougar stood near the horse with a dead man strapped on. "Let's see if we can get these animals taken care of. They've had a hard couple of days, but they're tough." Chance was grim, sad on the one hand, angry on the other, ending the chase, but not bringing his man to Judge Stanfield.

Chance and Cougar walked their horses and the mule into the barn while a squad of soldiers took Stokes' body to be prepared for burial. Raven joined them in the stables, offering coffee and some smoked venison. "Such a sad thing," Cougar said, slipping the saddle from his horse. "He is so young."

"What are your plans now, Cougar? I'll be riding back to Winnemucca, then to Carson City, and finally, home to Preston. They haven't got the telegraph wires stretched all the way to Preston, so Jennifer and Ben won't know about Jim until I have to tell them. It's gonna be a long slow ride." He slumped onto a barrel, sipping his coffee, worrying about how he would tell Jennifer such sad news.

"It will take me at least two weeks to get home because of the stops and work I'll have to finish at each stop. Might have to shoot a hare or two to keep my spirits up," he said, smiling for the first time in hours.

Chance and Cougar were joined by Raven and Captain Wells at Stokes's burial, a quiet ceremony that lasted just a few minutes. The post chaplain read from the bible, Chance spoke a few words, and the wooden casket was lowered into the frozen ground. There was very little talk on the way back to the main post, each keeping their thoughts and ideas inside. Chance and Cougar went to their quarters before supper.

***

Morning found the two men at breakfast, possibly for the last time together. "Where'd you get off to last night?" Chance asked as they took their seats.

"Captain Wells sent for me and we spent a couple of hours discussing my future. He offered me the position of chief scout for the area, and afterwards, I had to take a long walk. I have a good position with Captain Sou, but this is even better."

"Meaning you accepted the job," Chance smiled. "I'm glad for you, and it means you will be working closely with your brother."

"That's the best part, I think. I'll ride with you back to Winnemucca, part ways with Captain Sou and pack my gear. I told Captain Wells that I would take the job but I will not wear a uniform. I'm a Paiute and always will be."

"Our ride into Winnemucca will be long and slow, too," Chance said. "I love the idea of warm sunshine but it is what causes the ice we'll be breaking through. I wonder if we couldn't make some kind of tough leather wrap for the horse's feet and lower legs?"

"I'll bet Raven could do that," Cougar said. "Wrapping the rags helps, but some good harness leather would work better."

It took Raven a couple of hours to fashion the shin guards and the two and their pack mule started off toward the south well before noon.

Chapter Fifteen

Jerrod Stockton and Sheriff Alvarado climbed up the side of the hill to get a long look at the trail as it wandered up the east side of the Golden Valley. They had been following Gustaf and Whitman for several hours and noticed that they appeared to be stopping often. "That lady is hurt bad, Jose. We're going to have to catch up pretty soon or we might lose her." Stockton pulled a telescope from his jacket and aimed it down the very visible trail.

"He isn't trying to hide his trail in any way," he said, "and it looks like he's turning back north. He isn't going to go over these hills or through one of the canyons into the long valley. If he stays on this course, he'll be coming up on Toby's old place. We better get moving."

Clarence Toby was buying one of the ranches from Preston Miller, one of the many pieces of property involved in the fraudulent land sales scheme that brought Jacob Chance to the Golden Valley in the first place. That land was then declared open and available for homestead, and Cotton Phelps filed on it since it adjoined the property held by his new wife, the former Sarah Jackson.

"Cotton left Toby's pitiful cabin standing, using it as an equipment and tool shed, but he runs some fine cattle on the land. I wonder if Gustaf knows that cabin is there?" Stockton urged the group on, hoping to overtake the outlaw and his hostage.

"What I'm wondering," the sheriff asked, "is why Gustaf abducted Marcia Whitman? Everything he's done since coming here is confusing. Digging on other people's property, being angry at everything, shooting his partner. Nothing he does makes any sense to me."

"In some way, it all relates back to Colonel Dickson and Preston Miller, but I'll be damned if I know how," Jerrod Stockton said.

"Gold," is all Alvarado said, and that seemed as good an answer as any. He could remember the look in men's faces when California was over run with gold seekers, how the concept of law, personal ethics, and good manners often disappeared when gold was discovered, a new strike claimed, or an old one produces again. "Gold," he said again, "has driven more than one man mad.

"Our Gustaf, if we were able to check, is probably a known criminal in Denver, not a well-known brewer of fine beverages, and in some way has a connection to Colonel Dickson. He is not a thinking man," the sheriff continued, "but rather, one who reacts without the benefit of thinking."

"I've known men like that," Stockton answered. "They can be dangerous. Gustaf is always angry and if he simply reacts to a situation without understanding the possible consequences," Stockton paused in mid thought. "Well, hell, Sheriff, that's what we're seeing." He snorted in apparent anger, nudging his horse into a faster trot.

They were riding as fast as they dared, understanding that a worn out horse late in the day would be a serious hindrance if they found themselves in a race to capture Gustaf or save Marcia Whitman.

***

"I can't go any further, Gustaf. I can't," Marcia said, writhing in pain, weak from a tremendous loss of blood from the gash in her leg, and feeling as if she were about to pass out and fall off the horse. "Please stop."

"No," he snarled, and slapped her horse with his quirt, putting the horse in a fast trot. They rode another couple of hundred feet before Marcia Whitman did lose consciousness and fell to the ground in a heap. Gustaf grabbed her horse's reins and simply kept going, leaving her in the snow and ice.

"I don't need you now, anyway, woman. Die and be gone," he snarled, goading the horses into a fast trot. He did not have a plan, didn't really know where he was, and thought the best thing to do was find some place to hide for the night. He was on the eastern side of the Golden Valley, the Good Hope River to his west, and the main road north was on the west side of the river.

"They're all fools," he stormed, kicking his horse into a lope. "They have that gold and it should be mine. They found that gold before I could use the map I paid for. They will pay, every one of them. I'll burn that town to the ground, burn it all." He was raving to the wind in his dash through the valley.

He didn't seem to consider that Sheriff Alvarado and a posse would surely be chasing him, and stayed on a straight course, not trying to hide his trail in any way. Gustaf lived for many years in New York City, after arriving in this country as a youngster. His family had been from Austria, but were killed in a fire not long after they arrived. Gustaf lived with an uncle who was a drunk, and who beat on the boy regularly. Gustaf ran away as soon as he could and moved to St. Louis for a short time, and during the War Between the States years lived in Chicago.

He needed to get out of Chicago fast, following an attempt to run a fraudulent scheme designed to bilk money from veterans returning from the war. His escape took him to Denver, where indeed he did operate a brewery, and used it to gain access to some of the successful gambling and entertainment parlors in the city.

While in the process of delivering great barrels of beer, Gustaf and his helpers would also steal from the saloon's safes and cash drawers, and glom onto anything else that might be available. He was successful at this for some time before fingers started being pointed.

The sheriff and marshals in Denver would like to talk with him about several robberies that took place following the signing of contracts to purchase barrels of beer. His move to Preston was initiated by two things. Foremost was the possible buried gold, and then the demands from the Denver sheriff to come in for questioning. The timing of Mayor Stockton's offer of land for businessmen, if they come to Preston, and the sheriff's demands were perfect.

It was this background of always being in a large city that complicated his attempt to flee Preston's sheriff. That is, he knew nothing about wilderness, about reading the lay of the land, about taking care of himself in the wild. There was probably a vague thought in the back of his head that he would need fire, food, and shelter, but it wasn't first and foremost in his mind. It should have been.

It was late January, mid-winter, with a heavy snow pack on the ground. Night time temperatures had been at or below zero for the last couple of weeks, and a man not prepared would die from the cold overnight. Gustaf would need a warm fire, and protection from the cold, and he had nothing with him to build a fire, and only the clothes on his back. As mad as he appeared to be, he did seem to understand that he needed to find someplace to get out of the weather.

Gustaf continued on his course for another hour when he came onto Cotton Phelps' range and found the old cabin. He rode straight for it, dismounted and tied the two horses to a hitching rail. Revolver in hand, he barged right into the empty cabin, only to discover it was more of a barn than cabin. "No, no," he stormed. "No!" and he kicked at some shovels standing along the wall.

"Where is the food?" he stormed, seeing only ranch and farm implements. "This isn't somebody's house," he snorted, finally understanding. He walked back out, mounted up and rode off, simply leaving the other horse tied off. "I need some place with food, and a stove," he muttered, following a trail that led off in a northwesterly direction.

A frontiersman would have been comfortable in that old barn of a cabin. It was getting dark and the cold was bitter by the time he spotted a ranch complex some two miles distant. He rode close, dismounted and slowly walked the horse to one of the outlying buildings, a barn, tied the horse to a small tree, and slipped inside. He climbed to the loft and was able to look out onto the main ranch house, now well lit from inside.

"Two women," he muttered, seeing Sarah Phelps and daughter Georgia busy in the kitchen. "Where is the man?" He remained in the loft, watching for another half hour, finally deciding that there probably was no man, and climbed down, creeping across the broad open area toward the back porch of the house.

He stood on the porch for several minutes, listening to Sarah and Georgia, and being sure they were alone. "I haven't milked yet, Mama," Georgia said. "Have I got time before supper's ready?"

"Sure, honey, plenty of time. Cotton said he'd be late tonight, so it's just us for supper. He's with Jennifer Chance's crew moving some cattle onto better winter pasture. Dress warm, honey, it's cold out there tonight. Did you bring wood in for the fireplace?"

"Sure, did Mama. It's stacked up right next to the fireplace and a stack of kindling's there, too." Georgia put on her heavy winter coat and moved toward the door when it was suddenly kicked open and a large man with a gun in his hand crashed into the kitchen.

"Don't move, either of you. I will shoot you dead," Gustaf snarled in his guttural accent that petrified Georgia. He waved the gun at both women, forcing them to move toward the center of the large kitchen, near their dining table.

The room was cozy warm with a substantial fire burning in the large wood stove, and Gustaf moved to stand in front of the stove, feeling the warmth flood his body. The kitchen table was set for three, and two pots were bubbling on the stove. "Where is your man?" he snarled, pointing his revolver, first at the three plates, then at Sarah. "Tell me now."

***

"Oh, my God, is that Marcia's body in the snow?" Jerrod Stockton said, spurring his horse toward the body, with Sheriff Alvarado and the other posse members right alongside. "Marcia," Stockton yelled, jumping from his horse and rushing to her side. "Marcia, are you alive?"

She wasn't able to answer, but Stockton felt a pulse and her skin still had a bit of warmth to it. "Get a fire going, Jose. She's almost frozen to death." He picked her up and moved her off the rocks she had fallen into while Billy Bristol cleared some snow away for her. "She's hurt bad," Stockton said, easing her down, and carefully looking at the large gash in her leg.

Alvarado gathered sagebrush and whatever else he could find and worked quickly to get a big blazing fire started while Stockton cleared away the wound to Marcia's leg and started cleaning it. "Billy, grab my saddlebags. I have some stuff in there that will help her," he said, ripping more material from her already damaged blouse.

"That bastard just rode off and left her. Even took her horse," Alvarado said, kicking snow and rocks in his anger. "He will hang, Jerrod. I will bring him in alive just so I can watch him hang." He stemmed his anger somewhat by ripping more sage from the ground and throwing it on the growing bonfire.

Stockton had her wounded leg exposed, blood slowly draining from her body. He did what he could to clean the wound, and using strips of cloth closed the wound and tied more bandages around it. "I'm glad she's all but unconscious," he grumbled. "What I'm doing would hurt like hell if she could feel it."

Alvarado was pacing around, pulling more sagebrush for the fire, looking at the tracks of Gustaf's horses, and seeing the sun get lower and lower in the winter sky. "It's going to be a cold one tonight," he muttered.

"It looks like Gustaf's moving away from these hills to the east and back into the valley proper. If he keeps going that way, he's sure to run onto Cotton Phelps' place," Alvarado said. "As dangerous as that man is, God help them if he jumps them. Cotton won't know he's already killed and is running for his life." Alvarado was torn between leaving Stockton to care for Marcia Whitman and giving chase to Gustaf, and knew in his heart he had to stay with Stockton. "Is she going to make it, Jerrod?"

"I have the blood stemmed, but this lady is in bad shape," Stockton said, putting the finishing touches to bandages on her wounded leg. "She's dehydrated, lost lots of blood, and suffering from shock. Keep that fire going, Billy." He stood up and walked to his horse, untying his bedroll from behind the saddle.

"Help me get her tucked inside the wool blankets. We have to keep her warm, and hope she regains consciousness so we can get some water in her. Damn, Marcia, don't die on us, woman. Stay with us, Marcia."

Bristol and Alvarado gathered as much sage and other brush as they could and stacked it near the fire. "I think it's best if you go back to Preston, Jerrod," the sheriff said, putting more wood on the fire. "Let us continue tracking Gustaf. He's so dangerous, and riding toward the ranches, no one will know that he's a murderer, a monster."

"You're right, Jose. Go while you still have some light. I'll get her as warm as I can, bundle her up, and bring her back to town. If I can get her warmed up and get some water in her, she'll live."

He was stacking more sagebrush on a raging fire as Alvarado and the two deputies rode off.

Chapter Sixteen

Chance and Cougar rode through the remains of the massive blizzard, finally reaching Winnemucca in the afternoon of the third day. "I thought it was cold when we were riding into the storm," Chance said stepping off Mr. Morgan in the warmth of the town stables, "but last night was more than bitter." He tied off the horse and mule, and watched his big Indian partner tie his mount as well.

"We burned a lot of wood last night, Marshal," Cougar smiled, shivering a little with the memory. "What are your plans, now that we're back in town?"

"Close the books on the Winnemucca robbery and murders, make sure the books are closed on the Austin attempted robbery, and the murder and robbery in Ione, and then head for Carson City. I should be able to ride out in the morning, if the telegraph system is working. And you?"

"Find Captain Sou and wrap up my business with him, and head back to Fort McDermitt." He gave Chance a big smile, saying, "But I might wait until it's just a little warmer."

They walked up the street toward the Sheriff's office. "There's a really nice Basque Restaurant I was told about, right across from the hotel. Why don't we have supper together, Cougar. I don't want to just walk off in the middle of the street. We've had some interesting time together, and I want to remember our parting in a favorable way."

"That would be fine with me, Fists Like Iron." He couldn't hold the chuckles back, and the two parted company. "I'll see you at six, then," Cougar said.

"You come south to Preston, Cougar. I have a lot of friends I want you to meet. You're a fine man, and I'm proud to call you my friend."

Bear hugs in the middle of the sidewalk and hands clasped, the two men parted, nodding a mutual understanding two warriors feel without having to say anything. *I've lost a brother-in-law and made a friend,* Chance was thinking as he walked into the wonderful warmth of Alonzo Sanford's office.

"Chance," the sheriff said, jumping to his feet. "You're back," and he walked around his desk, reaching out his hand. "That storm must have been pretty tough on you and the Paiute. Were you successful?"

Chance shook hands with Sanford and stepped to the stove, cherry red and offering a pot of boiling coffee. He poured his coffee even before he slipped out of his bearskin coat. "We made it, Sheriff, and I don't think I've ever been as cold as I was last night. We were successful in that Mr. Stokes will never bother anyone again. He died from injuries suffered while we were chasing him."

Saying it that way, Chance figured, he won't stir a desire in the sheriff to get deeper into how Stokes died. Only he, the Army, and Judge Stanfield need to know how Stokes met his end. "After leaving here that fool stole a horse and shot and wounded a cowboy, and after a ranching family found him, injured and almost frozen to death, he terrorized them."

He shrugged out of his heavy bearskin coat and hung it on a peg alongside one of the sheriff's jackets, and poured another cup of coffee before grabbing a chair and moving it close to the stove. "That's better," he said, as the sheriff pulled up a chair next to him.

"It's best all-around that he met his end. I'll need to use some of your resources for the next couple of hours, Sheriff. I need to inform Austin, Ione, Carson City, and San

Francisco that the Stokes' episode is over so they can close their books. Are the wires still up and operating?"

"That's good news, Chance. Full service has been restored to the telegraph system. Is your arm injured? Looks like you're favoring it some."

"Damn fool soldier shot me, but that's a whole different story," Chance snickered, refilling his coffee.

"Well, now, my friend," Sheriff Sanford said, "you're not going to get away with that. Tell me the story. It isn't that often that a U.S. Marshal will get shot by a soldier."

Chance chuckled at the comment and spent the next few minutes relating how Sergeant Amster and he had fought, and then how the sergeant came to shoot Chance and in turn die from Raven's knife.

"Just blew you right out of the saddle, huh? Damn lucky that Raven was right there. Sounds like you and Eyes Like Cougar got along well."

"We did indeed, Sheriff, but it looks like you and Captain Sou will be losing the benefit of Eyes Like Cougar. The Army made him a pretty nice offer and he'll be joining his brother Raven at Fort McDermitt. I'd ride with that man, anytime."

"He's about the best that we have, Marshal. I'll miss his humor as well as his tracking ability."

Chance was able to notify all the agencies that Stokes was no longer a wanted man and they could clear the books on the matter. He finally got cleaned up at the hotel and met Cougar for supper. They spent hours telling and retelling their adventure, laughing over shooting hares, grimacing over wounds suffered, and making promises about keeping a friendship going for years to come.

"If you don't come to visit, Eyes Like Cougar, I'll put together a posse and chase you down," Chance said, and they parted late that night.

"I'll be there, Fists Like Iron," Cougar smiled, strolling down the dark main street of Winnemucca, shivering in the cold.

Chance spent the night in the hotel, had a hot breakfast, filled a pack with his valuables, added food and coffee to the pack, and was on the main road to Nevada's Capitol early in the morning.

The road west was the same that thousands of emigrants had followed since the discovery of gold in California. It was now a well-traveled thoroughfare, and Chance made good time, first following along the Humboldt River to the Humboldt Sink, across the feared forty-mile desert and then riding along the banks of the Carson River into Carson City.

It was cold every night, but a warm winter sun helped things along during the day. "All I want to do is get home, Mr. Morgan," he said often. Thoughts of Jennifer, Little Jake and the ranch made the journey seem even longer than it was. *The only time I'll be on the trail in the future is when that beautiful lady and I are driving cattle or horses. That badge is going to find a hiding place and I'll never look for it again.*

Along with thoughts of his family, Chance also spent time planning future changes and additions to their property. He was sure that he would be building a fine remuda of ranch horses, and they were already planning on increases in the cattle herd. *I remember the night I told Jenny I never even had a home to go to. She gave me hell about that, and look at us now. Amazing.*

"Look at that, Mr. Morgan," he said, walking his horse and mule down Carson Street. "That's the capitol of our state, right there." He stopped at the livery and stables, putting up his animals, and with his pack over his shoulder, booked a room at the St. Charles Hotel.

"It's over," he muttered, slumping down onto a soft bed. "I won't do this again. I need to be home with Jenny and Little Jake, not chasing outlaws, fighting blizzards, and dealing with idiots. I'm going home, and that's where I'm going to stay." Sleep came easy to the big man, who discovered to his dismay the next morning that he hadn't even shucked his boots.

***

"If I press hard, I'll be in Preston in three days, Ira, and then I'll have to tell Ben that Jim didn't make it. That will be one of the hardest things I've ever been faced with. I have come to love that old man."

"I think he'll look on it as a salvation, Jacob. He won't be tortured by the misdeeds of his son, and I'm sure he will spend a great amount of time with Little Jake."

"I hope you're right. Please come down to visit," Chance said, shaking hands with his old friend. "It would be some kind of party if you and Stan Martinez could be there when Eyes Like Cougar showed up. That crazy Apache and my Paiute partner would tell stories that would make our blood run cold, Ira.

"Jenny will chase you down if you don't show up come spring," he quipped, heading for the door. "I'm leaving right now instead of waiting until morning."

Chance had spent more than an hour with Judge Stanfield, going over all the details of the chase and the ending. "So, Marshal Chance," Stanfield said in his most judgelike manner, "you let a soldier sneak up on you and put a bullet in your arm. That's not the Marshal Chance I know," but he let a slow grin cross his face before actually laughing out loud.

"You got me on that, Judge," Chance said. "Never saw it coming, either. The only reason I'm alive is how fast Raven reacted. He had a lot of bitterness to wipe clean and did it with his knife. I raised hell with Captain Wells, you have to know."

The men shook hands, Stanfield promising a visit to Preston come spring, "Unless of course you have some criminal activity to bring before my bench."

The trail was pocked with patches of snow and ice, and the sky was blue and endless, with none of the harsh winter winds Chance had been fighting. Instead of taking the road through Bodie and over the White Mountains, Chance went south through that long empty valley and didn't have to face great drifts of high mountain snow. "I'll be so glad to put this badge away," he said, putting Mr. Morgan in a solid miles eating trot. He let his mind slowly come to a peaceful place, moving through scrub sage and cedar bushes.

Nevada's geography sometimes makes it relatively easy to move north to south or vice versa, with mountain ranges tending to be north/south with long valleys in between. Many of the ranges will have snow fed and spring fed streams emptying into those valleys. With the exception of one river, all of Nevada's streams and rivers empty into these valley sinks and lakes, making it convenient for travel on horseback. It is seldom that one finds one's self long distances from water or fresh grass.

The vast area known as Nevada is often referred to as a desert, but it isn't the open sand dune type of desert. Rather, the moniker should be high mountain desert, and the valleys between the ranges are often filled with growth. Maybe not lush, as in Kentucky, but plentiful grass and browse.

Chance let his mind drift through some of his early years in the Marshal Service, but his face had a decided smile thinking about Jennifer and the life he was building. *I'll never be able to work cattle as well as she can*, he was thinking, *or rope a steer at either end with ease. She can heel just as well as head a calf and I'm lucky to just hit the critter,* he smiled. *To ride with her when we move the herds is a learning experience I'll never tire of.*

His mind drifted through cattle drives up into the White Mountains in the late spring and back down to the Golden Valley floor in the late fall, and all the time he spent with his horses, breeding, training, remembering everything the Spanish Vaqueros had taught him.

Two years ago I was a saddle tramp of a Marshal, no home, dealing with far more criminals than nice society, and here I am, married, a father, and damn me, a rancher. Pappy would sure be talking fast if he knew that, and he found himself snickering out loud at the thought.

I haven't had thoughts of the old homestead, of my sister, and that wonderful old man, Pappy, for a long time. I want Little Jake to have good memories of his childhood on the ranch. I simply did not like living on that farm. What a difference there is between a dirt farm and a cattle and horse ranch.

"We've made good time, Mr. Morgan, but it's time to find a grove of trees or a rock overhang where we can have a warm fire and a good sleep." He spotted some scraggly trees and patches of green a few miles ahead and walked his horse the last half-mile in to let him cool out before stopping. "I've got some of Judge Stanfield's Kentucky in that flask, some of Ira Stone's smoked venison, and biscuits from the St. Charles Hotel, so all I need is a little warming fire and I'll have a banquet," he joked to himself, setting up a quick camp.

"Looks like a little spring there, Pal," he said to his big Morgan stud, "and fresh grass for you and the mule, and even some dried wood to get that fire started."

The sky was just showing some light when Chance was back on the trail on his third morning out. "I'll come into the valley from the north end, so I'll go straight to the ranch. Should be there in twelve hours or so if we keep steady, old man," he said to his horse. At a steady trot walk trot walk pace, he should do sixty miles or more, and he was estimating that he was about that far out.

***

Gustaf's eyes were wild as he surveyed the kitchen, waving his weapon around. "Where is your man?" he demanded for the second time.

"He'll be here shortly, Mr., and you'll be dead when he gets here," Sarah said, anger and fright giving her courage. "You better leave now. Get out," she yelled, moving toward a large cleaver on the sideboard.

"Stop," Gustaf snarled, stepping quickly in front of her. "I will shoot you. Now, fix me supper, and be quick."

During the small amount of time since Gustaf stormed the kitchen, Georgia had snuck out into the living room, and quickly dashed out the front door of the house, running to the corrals near the barn. It was already below freezing and she slipped several times on the ice getting to the corrals.

She found her favorite horse, saddled quickly, and rode hard toward the Chance ranch, about five miles away. *Mama said Papa Cotton was working cattle on the Chance ranch,* she remembered, driving her heels into the sides of her horse. "Come on," she said, "faster, please, faster." Tears were streaming across her face, crying from fear, and tearing up from the cold.

Gustaf heard the horse thunder away and was livid with anger, kicked a chair, and swung the heavy revolver at Sarah's head. She was able to duck away in time and tried to run for the door. He shot at her and missed, but it frightened her so much, she stopped running.

"Now, woman," he said, grabbing her by the arm and twisting her around to face him, "I want food." He slapped her hard across the side of the head, hard enough to buckle her knees, and she had to hold onto a chair to keep from falling. "Food," he snarled again.

She took a couple of minutes to gather her thoughts and try to calm down. *Georgia is safe,* she knew, *and she will bring help. Keep your senses, Sarah. Do what this mad man wants and don't let him hurt you.* Her mind was reeling with questions that she couldn't answer.

Is this the man Jerrod Stockton said would open a brewery? He's mad, and he's very dangerous. Why is he here? What has he done to bring him here? She was slow as she could get putting together a plate of food for Gustaf. "My husband will be here very soon, and he will kill you. Eat this and leave."

"Sit across from me, woman, so I can see you." He brandished his weapon, glowering at her. "What is your name?"

Sarah moved around the table and sat down, back a bit from the table, but didn't say anything. The night was getting cold and the only fire going was in the cook stove. The fire in the living room had not been lit yet and a chill was felt. "I need to light the fireplace," she said, starting to rise.

"Sit," he stormed, shoveling food into his mouth, as a mongrel dog might. "What is your name?" he demanded again. "You are making me angry, woman. Tell me your name."

"My name is Sarah Phelps," she said, sitting back down in the chair. "Why are you here?" she demanded. "You have no right to be here, and you better be gone before my husband gets back. He will kill you, Mister."

Gustaf ate like a pig, Sarah thought, watching the man slurp his food right off the plate. "Coffee," he said. "Make coffee."

"We don't drink coffee," she lied, not moving. "I need to light the fireplace. It's cold." She wanted to get into the living room where Cotton kept a rifle and shotgun near his big chair. The rifle was always loaded and she was a crack shot.

"You broke the back door, the wind is cold. I need to light the fireplace," she said again, starting to get up.

Gustaf exploded in anger, and jumping to his feet knocked his chair back against the counter. He reached across the table, slapped Sarah across the side of the head with his revolver, and she collapsed, unconscious, to the floor, bleeding from the wound.

"Damn woman," Gustaf said, getting up from the table and walking into the living room. He spotted the rifle and shotgun immediately and smiled, knowing why Sarah wanted to come to this room. He walked back into the kitchen, rifle in hand, and kicked at her body.

"Wake up, woman, and go light the fire," he said, laughing almost madly. "Up," he howled, kicking harder. Sarah slowly came to, sitting up, rubbing her head, finding fresh and dried blood. The room was spinning slowly, she couldn't seem to focus her eyes, and Gustaf kept kicking her, screaming for her to get up.

It took long minutes for her to be able to stand, and she saw he had Cotton's rifle in his hands. She slowly made her way to the living room, found the striker and lit a lamp. Slowly, she moved to the fireplace, wondering if she could use one of the iron pokers for a weapon, or maybe one of the logs. She stirred the still warm coals from the daytime fire, threw some kindling in, and placed a couple of logs on. *I'm too weak to attack him*, she finally understood, having trouble even getting the logs in the fireplace.

"You'll be sorry for hitting me, mister. My husband will kill you." She slumped into Cotton's chair, feeling something hard on her right hip. *I don't know what I'm feeling, but I hope it's a knife or a gun. I can't let him hit me again or I'll die. God, my head hurts.* She kept her eyes on him, and when he wasn't looking at her, she tried to feel around and find out what the lump was she was almost sitting on.

Her fingers curled around the handle of a revolver. *I'm so glad I married you Cotton. Hiding a gun under your cushion is just like you. Please, God, make sure this gun is fully loaded and ready to shoot.*

She had a good grip on it when Gustaf grabbed and jerked her to her feet. "Into the kitchen," he snarled, and she had to leave the gun under the cushion. He shoved her hard, and she stumbled and fell onto the kitchen floor. He put wood in the kitchen stove.

***

Jerrod Stockton had Whitman's wounds cleaned and bandaged, the bleeding was stopped, but she had lost so much blood that her condition was critical. "If I can get some water in her, I can get her back to town."

"I'm not going to give up the chase," Alvarado said, just before he and the posse moved out. "That man has killed one person, shot Randy, and now has almost killed Marcia Whitman. He is not getting away from me, Jerrod. You take Marcia back to town, but we're going to continue. It's almost dark, and we have lost a lot of time.

"I'll have a difficult time not just shooting him," Alvarado said, motioning for the two posse members to follow. "Keep her safe, Jerrod, and spread the word in town about what's going on. I'm worried that fool will stumble onto a ranch, and God knows what he'll do."

"When I get to town I'll send several men out to the various ranches to spread the word. Catch that bastard, Jose. You catch him."

***

When Whitman was finally warmed, she regained consciousness enough for Stockton to get some water in her. The huge blacksmith easily picked her up and cradled her as he stepped into the saddle. "I hope he can bring that bastard back to town, and maybe we will get some answers," he was thinking as he rode off toward town.

He spent the time riding to town talking softly to Marcia Whitman who seemed to come in and out of consciousness. "You'll be fine," he said often, along with, "Don't worry, I'll take care of you." For all his size and strength, Jerrod Stockton was a very gentle man. He is able to beat iron and steel into forms of beauty, lift wooden wagon wheels that weighed more than him, and still help in the birth of a lamb or calf.

After reaching town, Stockton took Whitman to her hotel and had a couple of the local women look after her. He went up and down the main street, spreading the word about Gustaf and gathering several men to ride with him. "We need to get to the Chance ranch, gather some of the cowboys there, and spread out through the valley ranches and help Sheriff Alvarado find this fool."

Within half an hour, nine men rode north toward the Chance ranch, led by Stockton. "When we get there, two of you take off right away for the Stokes ranch. Old Ben is there with just a skeleton crew this time of year, and might need some help."

Chapter Seventeen

It was mostly dark and the trails between the ranches were dim at best, seldom used by teams of horses and buggies or wagons. Georgia was having a hard time seeing the single track, but kept her pony in a solid canter, wanting to let him race, knowing she didn't dare. "Five miles, Billy Boy, that's all we need. Stay on the trail and we'll find Papa Cotton, and he'll kill that horrible man."

She was crying, sobbing, anger and fear racing through her body. *Did I do the right thing* she questioned, *running away, leaving Mama? Should I have stayed and fought that man?* Twelve years old, but remembering how Sarah had stood up to that horrible banker, Preston Miller, how she had spit in the face of Clarence Toby when he ran them off their ranch, gave her all the strength of an adult.

She let Billy Boy have his head as they raced through the night. The horse was raised and trained on the open range and side stepped the large bushes and leaped the smaller ones, and Georgia had learned to ride on the open range, and the two sped toward the Chance ranch.

Through the dim late winter moonlight, she spotted a small herd of cattle coming across a pasture off to her right and slowed Billy Boy to a gentle trot, not wanting to spook the cattle. *Papa Cotton is supposed to be moving cattle for Jennifer, I hope that's him. Please, God, make it be him,* she said, working through the sage and other brush toward the rear of the cattle herd.

Two cowboys rode toward her as she moved through the brush, and she waved at them. "What on earth are you doing out here at this hour?" Cotton Phelps shouted when he recognized her. "What's wrong?" he said as soon as he saw her tear stained face, and not understanding what she was blubbering at him.

"Slow down, Georgia," he said, lifting the girl off her horse and holding her close. "It's okay, Georgia," he cooed, gently stroking her hair. "What's wrong?" Fear gripped the rangy Phelps, not wanting to hear what Georgia was going to tell him, and afraid he was going to lose everything he had ever wanted.

"Mama," Georgia kept crying. "Mama."

"Take it easy, Georgia, nice and slow. Tell me what's wrong. What happened to make you ride out here tonight?" For all his size and strength, Cotton Phelps was a gentle man. Sarah always said he was the quietest, most gentle man she had ever known, with her, with Georgia, with all their animals, and that gentleness was evident as he calmed young Georgia down. "Tell me what's happened?" he pleaded.

Georgia's sobbing slowed and she wiped her face with her coat sleeve. "A horrible man with a gun broke into the house, Papa Cotton. I ran away as fast as I could to find you. Mama needs help."

Cotton gave her a big kiss on the forehead and set her back on her horse, calling to the other cowboy. "Get the boys and come to my ranch as fast as you can ride. Sarah's got trouble. Come on, Georgia, ride like you've never ridden before," and he nudged his big cow horse gently, spurring the animal into a full gallop in two strides. "Let's go."

Chance's foreman, Buck Colby spurred his horse back toward the main ranch to gather as many hands as possible. Jennifer and Chance kept just a skeleton crew during the winter months, so Colby would only be able to bring two, maybe three people on the ride back to Phelps's place.

The night had come fully on and with it, the icy cold of winter. There wasn't a cloud in the sky and the starlight danced and sparkled with the cold. Millions of pinpricks of ice glowed from every bush and blade of grass as the two sped through the open range.

There was just enough of a moon to give Cotton and Georgia some idea of where the largest of the sagebrush were, where the gullies were that they jumped, and where rocks were that they had to miss. The wind bit deep into their faces while lips and noses froze. Crystals of ice formed under their noses as they careened through the open fields of the Golden Valley, racing home, only thinking of Sarah.

Cotton had told Sarah so many times, "That girl rides like she was born in the saddle," and he was glad of that right now. *I will never allow another man to ever touch Sarah. What has happened?* he kept repeating in his mind. *Who would break into our home?* Flecks of foam flew from the horses and they sped through the early night, mindful of the dangers lurking under the horses' hooves, and the danger that might await them when they reached the ranch. A misstep or an unseen badger hole, and a horse and rider would tumble through the rocks and brush, and something to startle the racing horse could force a severe sidestep and toss a rider. There was danger on every step the horses took.

Hurry Papa, Georgia repeated with each lunge and jump Billy Boy took. Fright can produce an inner strength of immense energy, and Georgia was a very strong young girl as she kept up with Cotton Phelps the entire way to the ranch. *Hurry Papa, hurry,* she cried and moaned, over and over.

***

"Should see lights from the ranch pretty quick, Mr. Morgan," Chance said, trotting the big stud through deep grass and a light covering of snow, a couple of miles from his home. "It's been one long day, eh pal? You'll have fresh hay and maybe a touch of those oats you love pretty quick, old boy." They topped a small hill and he was looking down on his ranch house, about a mile away. "We're home, big boy. Home."

About five miles before, as the sun was already down, but he had moonlight to help guide him, he had debated whether or not to pull up and spend the night on the trail, coming in first thing in the morning. *It's one more cold night with little to eat, or tough it out and ride in in the dark,* he questioned. It was the thought of again holding Jennifer close, of rocking Little Jake, and of course, of sleeping in his own bed that made the decision fairly easy. "Come, on Mr. Morgan, we're going home," he snickered, nudging the big stud into an easy trot.

As he rode closer to the ranch he saw a tremendous amount of activity going on just outside the kitchen door. "Wonder what all that is?" he said, nudging the horse and pack mule into a lope, tendrils of anxiety making its way through his body.

He pulled Mr. Morgan to a stop and bailed out of the saddle just as Jennifer came out the back door. "Chance!" she howled, jumping off the last two steps and running as fast as she could to him. "Oh, Chance, you're home." She wrapped her arms around the big man, almost squeezing all the air from him, knocking his sombrero right off his head. "Oh, Chance, I've missed you," she sobbed, kissing him, hugging him, crying with joy.

Chance was squeezing back, rocking with her, and also, kept looking at all the activity. "What's going on? I love you, Jennifer. Why are all these men here?" Then he saw Jerrod Stockton and several more men ride into the ranch. "What's going on?"

Jennifer started to say something about Sarah Phelps when one of the Chance cowboys came over. "Glad you're back, boss. We have big trouble." He didn't get past that when Stockton broke in.

"'Bout time you got back," he smiled, whopping Chance across the shoulders. "We have trouble, Chance."

"Buck started to tell me. What about Sarah and Cotton?"

Buck Colby told what he knew about some man breaking into the Phelps's home and holding a gun to Sarah, about Georgia racing through the night to find Cotton, and the two heading to the ranch. Stockton jumped in and told about Gustaf going crazy, shooting Randy Beuller, killing Jeremy Lawton, and injuring Marcia Whitman.

"We better ride for Cotton's place now," Chance said, pulling Jennifer close. "I'll be back as soon as I can," he said with a rueful smile. "Damn," was all he said, stepping into the saddle and leading about twelve men out onto the trail to the Phelps' ranch. "I love you," he mouthed to her on the way.

Jennifer was crying, first because he was back, second because she knew he would always come to a friend's aid. *I'm the luckiest woman alive. Golden Valley is lucky too, that Chance lives here. If there's trouble, Chance will fix it.* She listened to the hoof beats dwindle in the distance and walked back in the house, still sniffling, wiping her eyes and nose.

Stockton rode up alongside Chance after the group got lined out and traveling at a good trot. "This is a hell of a way to welcome a man home," Chance smiled to his friend. "Sounds like this Gustaf feller might be slightly off center. Tell me about him."

Stockton told him the long story, and about the fact that Gustaf and Lawton may have been trying to find gold that Colonel Dickson may have buried. "Greed will do that to a man," Chance muttered. "I doubt Dickson or Preston buried any treasure, though. He was planning to run out on his people and take his gold with him. Sounds like some kind of fairy tale told by drunks in Denver."

"Gustaf is mad, Jacob, and he has no compassion. He just left Marcia to die. Just left her to freeze to death. He doesn't want me to get my grubby hands on him." Chance had to snicker at that thought.

"You'd just pick him up and throw him into the next county, eh Smithy?" he said, laughing at the thought. "Let's put these horses into a nice lope and get some miles under us," he said, nudging the big stud a bit. "Hope Cotton doesn't try to take that fool on without thinking first. A mad man is a very dangerous person. You said he shot Randy Beuller? Hell, Jim Stokes shot Randy, not Gustaf."

No, Jacob, Stokes shot him first, and Gustaf shot him too. Randy's one very angry storekeeper right now," Stockton chuckled. "He'll be fine, just sore and angry. What happened with Stokes? Did you catch him?"

"Dead and buried at Fort McDermitt, clear up near the Oregon border. I'll tell you the whole story when we get this over with. Tell me about Ben Stokes. I've been worried sick over that wonderful old man. Does he still blame himself?"

"He's been spending lots of time with Jennifer and Little Jake, and she has him back thinking like the Ben we know. He'll be okay, but he won't like what you tell him."

It got colder with every minute that skipped by, Chance was thinking, as they neared the Phelps's. "Let's go in nice and slow, as quiet as possible," Chance said, motioning the group to come to a walk. At a fence line a hundred yards or so from the farm house, he halted the men and they stepped off their mounts and tied them off.

As he moved the bunch closer, they ran into Cotton and Georgia, hunched down behind one of the wagons. "Glad you're here Chance," Phelps said, grabbing the big man's hand. "I saw Sarah through the window a minute or so ago, and I think she knows we're here. Don't know where that bastard is, though."

"Besides this door and the front door," Chance asked, "are there any other ways into the house? And," he said as an afterthought, "would any other way in be locked?"

Sheriff Alvarado and his two posse members snuck up behind the wagon about that time. "Chance, good to see you. Got back just in time." Chance and Stockton brought Alvarado up to speed and he and his two men moved around to the side of the house that had windows.

Jerrod Stockton spread the rest of the men out in a half circle around the back of the house, and sent three men to the front. It was very quiet, bitter cold, with just enough moonlight to allow the men to move about easily. "If he tries to run, we'll have him," Stockton said, slipping in behind the wagon.

"His horse is in the corral with ours," Cotton said, "unsaddled and eating hay. Even if he tries to run, he won't have anything to run with. No, Chance, the only doors are the front and the back. There is a trap door in the hallway that leads to the cellar, but it's covered with a rug and can't be seen."

"Make sure everyone is aware that Sarah is alone with that fool, Jerrod, and keep an eye on me." Chance, patted the huge blacksmith on the shoulder, and started moving very low and slow toward the back door of the ranch house, his rifle cocked and ready. He moved under the brightly lit window, stopping to listen, hoping to hear some kind of chatter from inside. There was no sound.

Chance moved slowly toward the back door, splintered and hanging loose on its hinges. *I don't dare move that door. The slightest move and the noise would be like crashing china.* He was almost on his belly trying to see into the house when Sarah came into the kitchen.

"You sit in front of the fire, Gustaf and I'll get your water," she said, sliding toward the back door. *It worked for Georgia, and I can run just as fast as she can.* She was just a few scant feet from the door when Chance jumped up, flung the door open, grabbed her, and literally threw her over his shoulder, running hard back to the wagon.

"Gotcha, Sarah. It's okay, quit fighting, you're safe." She didn't even see Chance when he burst in and grabbed her, and she started screaming and fighting him, all the way across the yard and to the wagon. Within seconds, they could hear Gustaf howling in anger and frustration, followed by gunshots fired off in any and every direction.

"I'll get you, woman. I'll kill you just like the ugly hotel woman. You stole my gold. I'll kill you." The screaming went on for several minutes, punctuated by gunshots simply fired at walls or windows.

Cotton Phelps and Georgia were tucked down behind the wagon when Chance and Sarah came sliding in, tumbling would be more accurate. "Put me down," she screamed, kicking and trying to scratch at Chance's face. "My husband will be here and he will kill you," she was a wildcat, and Chance finally had to release his hold on her.

"Actually, I'm right here, Sarah," Cotton said, gathering the horribly frightened woman in his arms. "It's okay, Sarah. It's me, Sarah," he had to say at least two more times before she was calmed down enough to recognize what had happened. "Chance grabbed you and brought you out. You're okay, now. Here's Georgia, so calm down and take it easy. You're safe."

When she saw where she was and whom she was with, she threw her arms around Cotton and gave him a bear hug he wouldn't forget. "Cotton, Cotton," she wailed, "Oh, thank God. Where's Georgia?"

"I'm right here, Mama," the girl said, putting her arms around Sarah. "Marshal Chance saved you."

Gustaf was in a rage when he realized what had happened. He lost his hostage, but never knew why he had even bothered to break into the house. He was cold, he remembered, that was it, and hungry. But now, now all he had was his own revolver and a rifle and shotgun belonging to Cotton Phelps. *There is no one here but me. I will take food and find their money. I need to put some food in a package, and I will leave this place.*

Chance moved Cotton, Sarah, and Georgia out of the way, sending them to the barn where Cotton could take care of the women. "Did you bring that scatter-cannon of yours?" Chance asked the Mayor of Preston, Nevada, knowing he could almost level the ranch house with a series of shots.

"You bet," Stockton answered, smiling, "but I doubt Cotton or Sarah would want me to use it. Do you have a plan?"

Chance nodded that, indeed, he did. "Buck," Chance said to his foreman, "get around front and keep those men out there from doing any shooting or talking, unless that fool tries to run. I want him to think that maybe he can sneak out the front. Keep it really quiet and I'll try to flush him toward you."

Buck Colby snickered a bit, gathering himself to make the move. "You mean the way Jennifer taught you to move cattle?" he asked through the snicker.

Chance chuckled, "Yeah, something like that," and Colby moved back into the shadows and worked his way to the front of the house. "This Gustaf feller isn't going to get the slightest chance, Jerrod," Chance said. "Right now, I don't think he knows that we're out here. He thinks Sarah was able to get away.

"I'm gonna get as close as I can and try to call him out. If you see him through that window, shoot him dead. If he comes out the door and he's holding a weapon, shoot him dead. Any questions?"

"Not from me," Stockton answered, kneeling behind one of the wagon wheels, the huge shotgun at the ready. Chance looked around to make sure everyone was still in a half circle around the back of the house.

"Gustaf," he hollered. "This is Jacob Chance, U.S. Marshal. Put your weapons down and come out of the house with your hands up. This will be your only warning. Come out now, with your hands up."

It was very quiet for what seemed like an hour, actually just a minute or two, and then the light in the kitchen was extinguished. Just moments later the window exploded as a shotgun blast was fired through it. The blast was followed by three quick shots from a handgun, and then silence. Chance could hear heavy footfalls from inside the house, and hoped that Gustaf would try to run from the front.

Chance crept through the darkness and gathered himself near that smashed door, hoping that the mad German would bolt toward him. He had his weapon in hand, crouched in the cold, listening.

Gustaf didn't try to bolt either toward the front or the back, instead running back into the kitchen and firing the shotgun again. Stockton saw the flash of gunpowder near the window and let go both barrels of his scattergun, knocking Gustaf clear across the kitchen, over the table, and plastering him against the far wall. Screaming in pain, the big German slowly slipped down the wall, crumpling onto the floor.

Chance was through the door and inside the house instantly, his big revolver aimed at Gustaf's head. "One little move, mister, just one, and I pump five shots through your head." He walked over and kicked the shotgun away and Gustaf instantly pulled his revolver. Two shots erupted, all but simultaneously, Gustaf dead in an instant, Chance hearing the whine as a large piece of lead narrowly missed his head.

Several men ran into the house, led by Jerrod Stockton. "Nice shooting, Mr. Mayor. He still had a little fight in him, but you put him against the wall with that monster scattergun." One of the men found a lamp and got it lit while a couple of others moved Gustaf's body out of the house and toward the wagon they had been hiding behind.

Alvarado and the men in the front of the house streamed toward the barn, some gathering horses and bringing them in. Lamps were lit in the barn, and the tension began to ease some.

"I was so worried, Mama," Georgia said, still clinging to her mother. "What a horrible man."

Sarah had not let go of Cotton, and just stood in the icy cold of the barn, hugging him as tightly as she could. "I knew you'd come, Cotton Phelps. I knew it. He hit me awfully hard, and my head hurts." She slowly slid down onto the ground, hugging Cotton's legs, crying softly.

***

The men dropped Gustaf's body on the ground at Alvarado's feet and Chance stepped away. "Bastard," he snarled, turned and walked into the barn, to where Cotton, Sarah, and Georgia were gathered.

"Sarah, old girl, you certainly know how to get yourself tangled up with outlaws, don't you?" he quipped, kneeling down at her side, offering a huge smile. "I'm sure glad you're as strong as you are. Your head okay?"

"It's fine, Jacob, just fine," she lied, then, barely smiling, said, "It hurts like hell, Marshal. Thank you," and she started crying again. Cotton Phelps held her as close as he could, and Georgia sat slightly to the side, holding one of Sarah's hands, crying and smiling at the same time.

"We heard gunshots," Cotton said, almost as a question. "Is anyone hurt?"

"Only Gustaf," Chance answered. "Jerrod Stockton's artillery piece peppered him pretty good. You'll have some carpentry work to do when we get out of your hair. You don't have a lot of windows left, and walls and doors got splintered some."

"It was really a surprise to see you, Jacob. When did you get back? We didn't know you were back."

Chance had to chuckle, thinking about the timing. "I rode into the ranch at the same time Buck Colby got there after leaving you, Cotton. I got off my horse, hugged Jennifer, got back on Mr. Morgan and rode here.

"It's nice to be home but I was expecting a little different greeting," he laughed, along with Cotton and Sarah. "I'm going to leave the rest of this mess up to Alvarado and Stockton, and I'm going home. I'm hungry, I'm tired, and I'm cold," he said, mussing up Georgia's hair, giving Sarah a peck on the forehead, and shaking hands with Cotton. "Most of all, I miss Jennifer. Good night."

"He's one hell of a man, Sarah," Cotton said, "and one hell of a friend. Let's get you back in the house, get that wound all fixed up, and get you in bed." He and Georgia got Sarah on her feet and shuffling through the mud and snow toward the house.

"Get those fires up and burning good, Georgia. I'll have to do something about the back door and those blown out windows, too. It's a cold one tonight."

"What a mess," Georgia declared when they got all the lamps lit in the kitchen and living room. She set chairs back on their feet, straightened the table back where it belonged, and stuffed some wood in the still hot wood stove. "I think I know what my chores are tomorrow," she smiled, kicking some broken glass out of her way. She pumped some water in a pan and put it on the stove.

Cotton put his arms around Georgia after getting Sarah's wounds cleaned up and her tucked in bed, walking back into the living room. "You are the bravest girl I've ever met, Georgia. You saved your mother's life, risked your own doing it, and became an adult in the process. I'm very proud to be your step-father."

Tears streamed across her face, already stained from several previous crying jags, and she hugged Cotton tightly. "I've been calling you Papa Cotton for two years, but I really want to call you just Papa," she whispered. "Is it okay?"

"I'll be so proud," is all Cotton Phelps could say, and the two stood in the living room, hugging each other, both crying like babies.

Chapter Eighteen

Sheriff Jose Alvarado and Mayor Jerrod Stockton, along with several people from town escorted Gustaf's body back to Preston. The men from Chance's ranch left with Chance, and Cotton's people worked to clean up around the outside of the house.

The mad German was bundled in the back of one of Cotton Phelps's wagons, and Stockton commented on the quiet.

"He hasn't been quiet since the day he arrived in town, Jose. Do you think we'll ever get answers to what drove him to do all these crazy things? If the word has been spread all the way to Denver that Dickson and Miller may have buried gold in Preston, he may just be the first to pester us. I think I'll rescind that offer of land for businesses, and only sell it after making some background investigations."

Alvarado snickered at the backtracking blacksmith. "Quite a change, there, Jerrod, but you are probably right. Dickson was the problem even though it was Miller, through his grandfather, who created the problem of land fraud. Dickson was a criminal through and through, and had contacts all over the west. We may be forced to live with whatever stories evolve from his time here."

It was early morning, no hint of sunrise yet, when the entourage arrived in Preston. Alvarado told his posse thank you and sent them home to their families, and he and Stockton got Gustaf into the jail. "Will he be okay until later this morning?" the sheriff asked, locking the cell door. "We'll bury him later in the day."

"I'm going to get all these horses and the wagon put up," Stockton said, "and then go to bed. What a day."

***

It was a long slow ride back to the ranch, and Chance fought bitter winds blowing icy cold into his face the entire way. "When I put the badge away this time, it will be the last time," he said, swinging down from the saddle. "Come on, Mr. Morgan, you need a good brushing and some fine hay. It's been a long ride, this time."

Jennifer left a lamp burning in the kitchen, but the sun was already declaring its intent as he walked into the house. He stirred up the fire and started a pot of coffee, doing his best to be quiet. He wasn't, and within minutes Jennifer had her arms around him, squeezing him just as tight as she could.

"I missed you, Marshal Chance," she said, over and over. "I was so worried, terrified that something dreadful would happen. Don't ever leave me again. Promise, Chance, promise."

"I just made that promise to myself, pretty girl. I'm Jacob Chance, rancher, from now on." He poured coffee for the two of them while Jennifer started putting together some breakfast.

"You must be hungry," she said, bringing out a basket of eggs and finding some potatoes and onions to fry up with them. She found some good side meat in the salt barrel and prepared it as well. Chance was slumped in his favorite chair at the kitchen table watching Jenny.

"I can't remember when I had something to eat," he laughed, shaking his head. "Mr. Morgan and I rode hard yesterday, and it's a good thing we did. While I was working to get Sarah freed tonight, I could only think of you. What if Gustaf had come here, threatened you and Little Jake, and I'm off chasing some damn fool criminal, instead of being here protecting you?

"No, never again. I will not leave you again." He stood up and snatched her away from the stove and hugged her tight. "I love you, little girl."

"After I get a pot of coffee in you, and a few pounds of food, I want you to tell me about Jim. Dad has been coming over almost every day, and Buck Colby has been keeping our cattle and horses, and taking care of Dad's ranch as well.

"Dad said the other day that he is sure Jim is dead, and I think he's finally admitting that none of Jim's problems are his fault. He hasn't come right out and said so, but I think he wants us to take over his operation too."

The conversation was ended with some squalling coming from the back bedroom, and Chance stood straight up and marched down the hallway, bringing Little Jake into the kitchen. "He's really grown in just these few short weeks," he said, sitting down, cuddling the little guy. "I've missed you, Buddy," he said, tickling him, making him giggle and squirm. "Strong, too."

Breakfast over, Jennifer demanded that Chance go to bed. "I have something very important to tell you, but not before you get a good rest. I have chores to do, and Buck Colby is waiting for me to line out his day. By the way, we also have a new hand that Hank Adams brought down from Carson City while you were gone."

"Juan Ortega is here? I wasn't expecting him until spring. This is good news, Jenny. Ortega is the finest Vaquero I could find, and our remuda will be the best." Chance wanted to get out and meet Ortega, but Jenny had other plans for the big man.

"Go to bed," she demanded, "and we'll spend the rest of the day bringing each other up to date," and she actually led him down the hallway to their bedroom. "I'll try to keep things at a dull roar around here for the next few hours," she smiled, closing the door on the way out. She thought she could hear snoring before she reached the end of the hallway.

***

"I'll take care of things around here, this morning," she said, walking into one of the corrals where Buck Colby was catching a horse. "I need you to ride over to Dad's and tell him that Chance is home, finally. Ask him to come over as soon as he can. You might want to tell him about all the trouble at Cotton's place last night, too. I imagine he's heard some of it already."

Colby saddled up and rode off toward the Stokes ranch while Jennifer and Little Jake started morning chores. "You're trying to walk, pal. You'll get the hang of it pretty soon," she smiled, watching him teeter this way and that, falling down every second or third step.

It took a few hours and the animals that were in corrals or pens were fed, the milk cow taken care of and eggs gathered, and Jenny was on her way back to the house, Little Jake riding on her hip, when Chance came out onto the porch.

"Morning," he said, stretching for the clouds, scratching at a four day beard. "Slept like a baby, in my own bed. I love that bed," he said, patting Jennifer on the bottom and sneaking a kiss, too. "I'll get myself put together and you can show me all the changes that have been made while I've been gone."

"We're a couple of weeks from calving, so you'll see some mighty fat heifers walking around those fields out there," she said, "and your horses have been asking about you every day," she winked, smacking him on the shoulder. "Go get prettied up and I'll give you the tour. Oh, by the way, morning ended a couple of hours ago."

She walked out to the corrals and found Ortega walking through a corral full of colts and fillies, letting the horses nuzzle him, brush up against him, and filling their lungs with his personal aroma. "Good morning, Mrs. Chance," he said. "Buck Colby said the Patron had come home. I'm excited to see him again."

"Yes, Juan, he got in late last night. He'll be here in just a few minutes. Looks like you've made some friends already," she snickered, watching the horses gathered around the Vaquero. "Are you settled in? Is there anything you need?"

"Everything is fine, thank you. Buck has me in with the other two hands in the bunkhouse. That's a very good stove in there, and I'm glad," he smiled. "We don't get cold weather like this in California."

"Here comes Chance, now," Jennifer said, nodding toward the ranch house. "I'll head back and let you two talk horses," she said, walking up to Chance. "When you get through with Juan Ortega, come get me and we'll take that ride through the cattle." She got another strong hug from Chance and took Little Jake up in her arms and walked back to the main house.

***

"This is the first crop from those brood mares I brought up. What do you think?" Chance asked as he and Ortega walked through the corral. "Wish you could have ridden with us when we brought them in. It was a good ride, though, across the Southern Sierra Nevada and up the Owens Valley."

"This is the start of a fine remuda, Don Jacob," Ortega said. "These are the two year olds? We will begin their work right away." He climbed through the rails of the fence and stood looking at the young horses. "I would have enjoyed that ride. Any trouble coming up the valley?"

"Had to chase off some Indians a couple of times," Chance said. "It was a good ride and proved to me that we bought the best horses. They showed stamina and strength, and once we got them here, they took to the climate and food.

"That crop of young ones you were working prove that point. About that Mr. Chance stuff, Juan, we're not too formal around here. Just call me Chance." He pointed out a few of the horses, and continued. "Most of these have had halters on and been walked under lead. I've ponied most with halters, and they respond to them, as you can see."

"I brought many of the hackamores that you liked," the Mexican horseman said, and some of those Mexican saddles you like, as well. Mr. Adams was very helpful getting me down here with everything. Marshal Martinez, the Apache Indian friend of yours made me promise to say hello from him, too."

"I'm glad you got to meet him. One of the best men I've ever worked with. Were you able to get some winter clothing? I guess you've noticed this isn't the same as Tehachapi country."

"Hank Adams took me to a couple of stores in Carson City, so I'm fine, and you bet I've noticed the cold. When do you want us to start working these young ones?"

"Let's plan on starting our work first thing in the morning, Juan. I'm going to spend the rest of today with Jennifer and the baby and get myself rested a bit from that long chase. Take your time and get to know the layout of the ranch, I'm sure you've met all the hands, and we'll meet right here in the morning."

They shook hands and Chance walked back to the ranch house, grabbed a quick gulp or two of coffee, and brought Jennifer and Little Jake to the barn to saddle up for the tour of the ranch. "I've never been happier in my life, Jenny," he said, sneaking a quick kiss and giving her a little pat on the bottom. "I'm home."

Chapter Nineteen

Jerrod Stockton and Juan Alvarado were at the Crystal Saloon having a cold beer following Gustaf's simple burial, attended by just them and Justice of the Peace Roger Bullis. "I'm glad we kept it as simple as possible. I'll send a notice to the sheriff in Denver even though that fine gentleman never answered my previous notes to him," Alvarado said.

"At least we don't have a Gustaf problem anymore," Stockton said. "He was disruptive in every way around here. It'll take some time to get the town back on an even keel."

"Here is what I found in the hotel room," Alvarado said, handing some papers to Stockton. "Looks like someone in Denver was selling maps where Dickson had buried some gold. About as phony as anything I've ever seen."

Stockton went through the papers, actually laughing a couple of times. "Either Gustaf or Lawton should have recognized immediately how fake these maps are. This isn't a map of Preston, it's just a drawing of a river going somewhere. Damn. Jim Stokes is dead, that fool kid Sparks Thomas and Jeremy Lawton are dead, Marcia Whitman won't be well for months, and Randy Beuller will be limping for a long time, all because of these stupid maps.

"You'd think that a man who knows how to brew good beer would be smart enough to see fraud," he stormed.

"It actually gets worse," the sheriff said, showing Stockton another piece of paper. "This is from Stokes to Gustaf. They had something planned before Gustaf got here."

"Let's do what we can to keep this from Ben. He doesn't need to know this." Stockton took the letter and crumpled it up, and walked to the big iron potbelly stove, watching it burn.

One of the town kids stuck his head in the batwing doors, announcing that the monthly supply wagon had arrived. "Good," Stockton said. "Let's go see what Dusty has for us this month." When they got out on the street, they found several other people heading for the livery, where Dusty always stopped first.

"Will you look at that?" Eileen Sprague said, pointing toward a large wagon with four mules in harness.

"Hey, Dusty," Jerrod Stockton hollered, "looks like you're coming up in the world. That wagon is about twice as big as what you usually drive, and four up, too. Getting' pretty fancy, there."

Dusty had smiles all over his face, his eyes crinkled up, nose twitching, and mouth spread all the way across his broad mug. "Gonna be some changes, Jerrod. Give me a hand getting' this thing unloaded and I'll tell you all about it."

Boxes and crates, gunny-sacks and baskets filled the back of the large freight wagon, and last out was the mail sack, which Roger Bullis hauled over to the hotel for distribution. "We'll be coming down twice a month starting with today's delivery, Jerrod," Dusty said as the group traipsed back to the Crystal. "Better than that, we renewed our mail contract, and we'll add a mail stage twice a month as well. How about that?"

"You are full of good news, old man," Stockton smiled. "That's the best news we've had around this old town for a long time. Is there enough business to keep two wagons and two mail stages moving to Preston twice a month?"

"Looks like it to me," the old teamster said. "This hits the spot," he said, taking half a pint of cold beer down in one swallow. "Wanted one of these last night, and the night before, too," he cackled. "Old Tiny still laid up, I see."

"That bullet did some serious damage, I'm afraid, Dusty. He comes down to the bar once a day, but runs out of energy fast. He'll be fine in another few weeks. What's the big news in Carson City?" Stockton was excited by the news of increased supply delivery, and an extra mail run, too, and wondered if something happening in the capitol had anything to do with it. "Something cooking up north we haven't heard yet?"

"Not really," he said. "Mines are doing well, the agriculture outlook in the Eagle Valley is good, the new stockyards that Hank Adams is working on are coming along. Between Golden Valley and Eagle Valley, northern Nevada folks are gonna be eating well," he laughed.

A stranger stuck his head in the saloon door, spotted the group at the table in the back and sauntered over. "One of you gents be Jerrod Stockton?" he asked, with a friendly smile on his face. "Hello, Dusty. Found your beer, I see." The gentleman was wearing what would be considered 'city clothes', such as starched shirt front under a wool vest, and tweed trousers instead of canvas, and had a pair of high top lace-up shoes on, instead of boots.

"Ah, Mr. Watson, hello," Dusty said. "Jerrod, Sheriff, meet Tyrus Watson, late of St. Louis. Ty, say hello to the Mayor and the Sheriff."

Hands were shaken, beer was poured, and Tyrus Watson got right to business. "Here's a letter for you, Mr. Mayor, from Judge Stanfield in Carson City." Jerrod took a large envelope and opened it to read several densely written pages, hemming and hawing, and finally smiling, set the pages down.

"A newspaper, eh? Well now," he said, settling back in his chair, taking a long draught of cold beer, and shaking his great head. "That's really good news." He handed the letter to Alvarado, and continued. "We have a couple of empty store fronts available, Mr. Watson, and we've had enough dumb and stupid things happen around this little village lately to keep you in business for some time to come." There was just a hint of humor to what Stockton was saying, and Dusty was sitting, rocking back and forth, chuckling up a storm.

"The judge pretty much brought me up to date on some of what you folks have been living with. I missed meeting Marshal Chance by just a few hours. He left Carson City just before I started looking for him. I'm looking forward to meeting that man."

"Without that man, you wouldn't have a town to set up business in," Alvarado said. "Tell us about yourself and your plans for this newspaper."

"I got my start in St. Louis," Watson said, "as a printer's devil, you know, just cleaning iron type, and then cleaning more type, and cleaning enough that I have printer's ink running in my veins. I came west to Nevada because of what I read about the fabulous Comstock Lode and the riches of Virginia City." He stopped for a minute for a quick sip of beer, and continued.

"I worked at the *Territorial Enterprise* with Dan DeQuill and that really funny writer, Mark Twain, but wanted to get out of the big city and start my own enterprise. That's when Amos Stanfield started telling me about Preston, and helped me acquire all the necessary equipment and supplies to get me started.

"I'm going to call my weekly paper *The Preston Leader*. Do you like that name? I do," he said.

"That's a fine name, Mr. Watson," Stockton said. "*The Preston Leader*. I like that. I hope there's enough advertising to keep you in business."

"I think you'll find there will be. I have another letter for you, but I wanted to get my information out first," he said, giving just a hint of a blush. Watson was a small man with reddish blond hair, cut rather short. His complexion gave one the impression that the man had never seen an hour in harsh sunlight.

He had long thin fingers, elegant, almost feminine, but a closer look revealed the dark stains of ink around the nails and cuticle. The man probably didn't weight one hundred twenty five pounds and it was doubtful he could spend a full day in the saddle. "I think you'll enjoy what is in this second letter very much, Mayor.

"If you folks don't mind, I'm rather tired from this long journey, and I don't believe that Dusty is a very good camp cook," he nodded to the teamster who just shrugged it off. "I'm going to grab a bite to eat at the café, take a nice nap, and then maybe, you can show me a place or two where I can set up shop."

Stockton, Alvarado, and Dusty watched the slim man walk out the door. Stockton said, "I hope he's got a little more strength than what I saw. This is pretty rough country for what I would call a tender-foot."

"What's in the letter, Jerrod," Alvarado asked and motioned for Chester, helping Tiny out behind the bar, to bring fresh glasses of cold beer.

"If I thought the idea of a newspaper might be a little bit strange, I mean, we're a small village with few people and not a lot of business, the judge has outdone himself now. It seems as though one of the banks in Carson City wants to open a branch in Preston."

"That's wonderful," Alvarado exclaimed, but was interrupted immediately by Stockton.

"Wait, Jose, that's just the beginning. Along with the bank, there will be a stock exchange partnership, dealing in particular with mining stocks and agricultural enterprise." Stockton sat back, shuffling the pages of the letter, looking all around the Crystal Saloon, almost in awe.

"I don't know, Jose. I just don't know what to say. A newspaper, that's one thing, and something that will be appreciated by all of us, but a bank? And a stock exchange?"

Dusty piped up next, before Alvarado could comment on the idea of a bank in Preston. "They are pushing the telegraph lines south to Bodie right now, Jerrod, and by this time next year, if I might add my two cents, you'll have a telegraph office in Preston as well." He snickered a bit before continuing. "That might put a cramp in my mail runs."

"I don't think so, Dusty," Jerrod said. "If we have a newspaper, a bank, and a stock exchange, you might have to increase that mail contract. I'm going to call a town meeting so everyone will know what's going on. Looks like our Mr. Watson will have some big stories to kick off his newspaper."

Chapter Twenty

For several hours, despite the cold, Jennifer gave Chance a complete tour of the home facilities, open pastures, fenced pastures, and more than one hundred very pregnant heifers. "It's almost the end of February, Chance, and these girls will be dropping calves starting in just a few weeks. Before the end of March, maybe a little beyond, we will have doubled our herd.

"Between our cattle and horses, and the crops that I've already got planned, this little homestead of ours is gonna be so full of life, it'll be amazing. We'll need several more hands before our spring drive.

"With our herd, Dad's large herd, and that good sized bunch that Cotton and Sarah have put together, you'll learn what it means to drive near a thousand head a couple of hundred miles, my friend," she smiled.

Chance was just a little contemplative for a minute before asking, "Have you had any trouble with Buck Colby or that Campbell fellow? You know, you being a woman. Have they done as you asked or made rude comments?"

"No, not at all, Chance," she said. "Both men are cattlemen and they know that I am too. You can put that right out of your mind," she gave him a big smile as they continued their ride.

They were working their way back toward the home ranch, still a couple of miles out. "You're right," Chance said, "those are nice fat heifers. We'll plan on holding back a considerable number of the new heifers again this year, just like we've been doing. This herd is growing fast, Jennifer." Chance had the look of a pleased and contented man as he gazed across the open grassland.

"Back on the farm, when I was a little kid, we didn't think about building or increasing the size. The farm was the size it was and you just planted so much. This is so different, and exciting. You've done this with your father, so it isn't new, but I'm enjoying this so much."

"It's different doing it with you, Chance. I'm just as excited as you are. You're sure you're not missing the badge?"

The big man just snuffed some, scowling at her. "I promised myself, about a thousand times while I was chasing your brother, that I would never put that badge back on, ever. That's a promise, Jenny." They rode in silence for a while, enjoying a late winter's day in a beautiful valley.

***

"That river is running high this year, Jenny, and with all the snow and rain we've had, we'll not be short on water. That heavy snow up high will take a long time to melt off. I want to bring the horses in from the open pasture and put them in fenced pasture real soon. It's time to put some work into them." His small remuda was growing as well, and he was anticipating a full season of training the colts and fillies that were now coming three years old.

The ride through open country had invigorated both Jenny and Chance, and even Little Jake was full of it, riding with Jenny. "Did you say you expected Ben to come by today?" Chance asked.

"I sent Buck over to help him move some steers and told him to tell Dad that you were home and to come by. He should be coming soon. There's something we need to talk about before he gets here.

"Let's ride over to that stand of cottonwoods and sit in the sunshine for a few minutes."

When she rode to check on the cattle and horses, Little Jake always rode with her, wrapped in a blanket that was slung across her front. "This little guy giggles up a storm when I put Chuckles into a full gallop. He loves it. He's gonna be a fine buckaroo, just like his mama," she laughed, handing him down to Chance.

She spread his blanket and laid the baby on it, wrapped tight against the early spring chill, and the two sat across from each other with Little Jake in the middle. "You sound like there's something serious going on," Chance said, passing a canteen over to Jennifer. "Is there a problem I need to know about?"

"It's certainly not a problem, but there is something you need to know about. Just about time for the fall roundup we're going to have another baby," she said, just calm as all get-out. "That means you have this spring and summer to learn everything there is to know about running a round-up, pardner," she laughed.

Chance sat absolutely still, half a grin on his face, the canteen hanging in midair. "Oh, my," is all he could say, over and over, still grinning like a little boy. "You're sure?" he finally managed to get out.

"Oh, I'm sure," she said, reaching out for the canteen. "Actually I was sure before you left, but that would have been so unfair to burden you with while you were chasing men that shoot people."

"That's the best welcome home I could possibly have," he stammered, still just staring at her with that little boy grin. "Does anyone else know?"

"No, I wanted you to be the first." She took a long drink of water, gave a little to the baby and handed the canteen back to Chance. "What are you going to tell Dad when he gets here?"

"The truth. It wouldn't be right to tell him anything but the truth. Jim wasn't right in the head, made some horrible decisions, and paid for them. It isn't anyone else's fault, and Ben cannot blame himself."

"I know Jim is gone, but I can't remember exactly what you told me earlier. I'm so excited by you being here. Did you actually catch him?"

"No," he said, shaking his head, slowly. "He was always just about a day ahead of us. You would like Cougar. He and I rode together after Jim's bank robbery in Winnemucca. We couldn't close the gap, and with a furious blizzard beating us up for several days, we actually lost him.

"He ended up at a ranch, all busted up with a broken arm, no food or water for a couple of days, and unconscious. After the rancher and his son took care of him, he turned on them too. Jim died from a severe blow to the head when he tried to hurt the old man. The son was built like a mountain and smashed him with his shotgun, then tried to nurse him as they rode toward Fort McDermitt.

"That boy was something, for sure." Chance's eyes were dancing as he described Jack McNaughton to Jennifer. "He was much taller than me, outweighed me by a bunch, and I swear, that boy would have been able to lift a horse if he tried.

"His father raised him to do the right thing, so hear this, Jenny. Young Jack McNaughton finds Stokes with a broken arm, passed out and clinging to a stolen horse. McNaughton brings him home and nurses him only to have Stokes try to kill him. Then, bringing him in to Fort McDermitt, Stokes tries to hurt the kid's father, the kid bashes Stokes, then again tries to nurse him back to health.

"I want Little Jake to grow up to be that kind of man."

She smiled, reached across and kissed him gently. "With you as his guide, Jacob Chance, our boy will be a perfect gentleman at all times."

Chance told her about Cougar and his brother, Raven. "I think Cougar could track a wisp of wind if he tried," he laughed, "and Raven saved my life big time."

He didn't go into detail on being shot by Sergeant Amster but did tell how Raven jumped in the middle of the fight and stabbed the sergeant. "That could have gotten messy fast, an Indian killing a soldier, but Captain Wells stepped in and stopped anything further from happening. Some people don't seem to understand that the Indians aren't that much different than us. Each is an individual, and the tribes too, are different from each other.

"You can't just put them all in the same barrel. That's what Amster did, and it got him killed." He got a little grin on his face, and continued. "Promise me you won't tell anyone about this, but because of the fight I had with Amster, Raven started calling me Fists Like Iron."

"I don't think I'll promise not to tell," she smirked, laughing, "Did you hear that, Little Jake. Your papa is called Fists Like Iron, so you better behave." Chance was almost blushing, scowling, and finally, chuckling along with her. "Is your arm okay? Is there something I need to worry about?"

"The doc said I need a good pour of whiskey in my coffee after supper, for the next ten years," Chance said, trying not to laugh. She cuffed him a good one, mouthing, 'Fists Like Iron.'

He grabbed her tight, and rolled her over, lying gently on top of her. He looked deep into bright eyes, and kissed her long and sweet. "Not in front of our boy," she whispered, but not trying to stop him at all.

"We'll save the rest for later tonight," she said, brushing some hair out of his eyes, letting him enjoy her mouth, his hands getting a little too busy. "Later, Marshal Chance," she finally said, taking his hands in hers.

They sat quietly for some time, enjoying the peace and quiet, and gazing at the late winter, early spring sky; so blue it almost hurt to look for any length of time. Fleecy white clouds billowed across the vast expanse of the Golden Valley, and they could hear heifers bawling in the distance. Little Jake was happily making baby noises on his blanket, crawling around, and trying his hardest to stand up. "He'll be walking soon, Chance, and I'll bet he will be a terror on two feet," she said, helping the boy to his feet.

"It's times like this that I didn't have when I was a boy on a farm back in Missouri," Chance said, leaning across the blanket and grabbing a quick kiss from Jennifer. "Dirt farming and cattle ranching are really different. I don't ever remember not having something that had to be done.

"Last summer, even when I was helping you move the cattle, we took the time to see where we were, enjoy this vast country we live in. I don't ever remember doing that as I was growing up." They spent another half hour under the cottonwood trees, and finally got saddled for the ride back to the ranch.

"I'm not looking forward to talking to Ben about Jim," Chance said. "It's going to be the hardest thing I've ever done. I told Cougar, and I know I've told you, I have come to love that man like my own father, and I'm going to tell him something that could break his heart.

"Let's make sure there's a good fire going, plenty of hot coffee, and try to keep things as positive as we can," he said as they rode toward the barn. "I'll put the horses up and you take care of Jake and the fire."

"I asked Cookie to roast one of Jerrod's geese. Let's not let Dad insist on going home tonight. We have room here, and I'd like to be close to him." Jennifer almost had tears running as she and Little Jake walked toward the big house.

***

Buck Colby and Ben Stokes moved a small bunch of cattle onto fresh pasture and then started on the ride to the Chance ranch. "You said that Jacob looked good and healthy, eh?"

"He sure did. He rode the entire day and got to the ranch in time to join us in our fight to save Sarah. He's one hell of a man, Mr. Stokes. Best man I've ever ridden for, and I've worked for some of the best. I don't think he's afraid of anything."

"He's changed some in the last couple of years," Ben Stokes said. "He's just as tough and strong, but his edges aren't quite as sharp. He's softened, just a bit, being a husband and father.

"Did he say anything about Jim?" The old man wanted to believe that Jim was safe, that Chance had caught him, but he knew better.

"No," Colby lied, not wanting to say anything. "We were pretty busy with the problem at Cotton's place. That Gustaf fellow was crazy. Jerrod Stockton shot him and Chance killed him and got him out of the house. He saved Sarah first. There wasn't much talking."

"I'm glad Sarah's okay," Ben said. "It sounds like the man must have been insane. You said he was in Preston to find gold? That's really strange."

"What Stockton and the sheriff both said was, Gustaf had been told that Colonel Dickson had buried a bunch of gold in Preston, somewhere along the banks of the Good Hope River."

"That's nuts," is all Stokes said. At a solid trot, the ride took about an hour and they tied off late in the afternoon. "I've got chores to do," Colby said, shaking hands with Stokes. "Nice riding with you." Ben whacked the young man on the shoulder and walked toward the house that he helped build, just a few years ago.

Jennifer, holding Little Jake met him at the kitchen door, getting a warm hug. "Hello little buddy," Ben said, taking the baby in his still powerful arms. "You come with your Grandpa, cuz we have places to go in this big world." Little Jake cooed and grinned, and Grandpa Ben did the same thing.

"Look at them, Chance. Little Jake looks like Dad and like you. He's the best medicine for Dad, right now." She and Chance stood and watched the two play and talk to each other. "You better go get some wood, old man. It's gonna be cold again tonight and I think we might be up talking for hours."

Chance headed out the door while Jennifer, Ben and Little Jake made their way to the living room after Jennifer poured coffee for them. "Chance will be back shortly, Dad. He's getting a good load of wood in the bin. I haven't been doing a very good job of that."

"Are you okay?" he asked, getting a worried look on his craggy face. "Please tell me there's nothing wrong."

"Just the opposite, Dad," she said, as Chance came back in with an armload of oak and pine for the fireplace. "We'll tell you all about it, won't we Chance."

He stacked the wood next to the big rock fireplace and shook hands with his father-in-law. "You look good, Ben. Just like a grandfather should look," he smiled, sitting next to Jennifer. "My wonderful bride gave me the good news just this afternoon, sir. You're going to be a grandfather again," he said.

"Wonderful," Ben Stokes said, reaching for Jennifer's hand and giving it a good squeeze. "Is there any good news about Jim?" he asked, settling back with his cup of hot coffee. "It's okay, Jacob. I can take it, but I do need to know the truth."

"I'm afraid there isn't any good news, Ben. Jim turned bad and stayed that way right up to the end. He was gone before I got to him, but I was able to see to it that he got a dignified burial at Fort McDermitt. Captain Wells saw to it and I attended."

"Thank you, Jacob. It's been difficult, but I think I've come to accept that Jim just wasn't the man I hoped to raise. I'm still not sure that I couldn't have done more, but I do realize that it's all water under the bridge now. What's happened has happened, and I must get on with my life."

They sat in front of a blazing fire, sipping hot coffee, nudged just a bit with some fine Kentucky, and talked about the ranches, about cattle and calving season coming up soon, and about Sarah and Cotton Phelps. It wasn't long before talk centered on the new addition to the Chance family.

"What will you name him?" Ben asked, and Jennifer jumped right on him.

"Maybe you mean her?" she questioned.

"Maybe I'll just put some wood on the fire," Jacob laughed, not getting into that discussion. "Although, Benjamin Chance sounds awfully good to my ears."

"Well," Jennifer said, "if it is a boy, I would like to have him named after his father. We will call him Fists Like Iron, Jr.," she laughed, nudging her father.

Lives were saved when Cookie stuck his head in and said, "Dinner, folks, come and get it while it's hot."

"My goodness, what a spread," Ben said, helping Jennifer to her seat. "While we enjoy this wonderful night, I want to talk to you about something else that's very important to me. When Jennifer, Jim, and I moved here from St. Louis so many years ago, and I built my ranch, and raised my kids, I had plans on being able to watch those kids end up owning and running that big spread.

"Life throws things at you, bounces rocks off your head, puts mud in your boots to slow you down, and trips you when you're not watching, and then, all at once, you find yourself at that point when it seems to be the right time to slow down and quit fighting.

"No, no, don't get all excited, I'm not gonna quit, but I am gonna slow down. That big old Stokes spread needs some young blood to keep it going, and I have a plan. I want to sit in my rocker on the veranda and watch each and every day come and go, see herds of cattle and horses and sheep move through those fields and pastures, and watch my grandkids get big and strong.

"I settled on one section, six-hundred-forty acres when we moved here, and thankfully, Amos Stanfield said my deal with Preston Miller, while fraudulent on Miller's part, was legal on my part. You two have half a section between you, so with the ranches combined, and so much fine range land for summer grazing, you should be able to maintain at least five hundred to a thousand calves a year, if you can get them to a market."

"Hank Adams has pretty much got us into the northern Nevada markets, Ben. He's putting in a stockyard and probably a processing facility for slaughter. That man's a go getter." Chance sat back with a grin on his face. "He was your best hand, Ben, and you sent him off to Carson City." Ben nodded, smiling, and continued talking.

"Now," and it was obvious that Ben Stokes had been preparing this little speech for some time, "for this to happen, somebody has to run the place. I, therefore, being of sound mind, name you, Mr. and Mrs. Jacob Chance, as the new owners of the Stokes Ranch. You, in turn, will give me life-long privileges of being able to live in my home, and help at any time I so desire or you so need my service. Sign here," he finished, flourishing a legal document he had hidden inside his shirt.

"Well, now," Jennifer exclaimed, "aren't you something. You've obviously been doing something besides sittin' and a rockin'. Chance, say something."

Chance stammered a couple of times, did some humming and catching of breath, and finally simply said, "Thank you."

The evening continued in front of the fireplace for several more hours, some of the time taken up with plans on coupling the two ranches and herds, some on raising children, and some on just being a loving family with good and bad memories. "Here's what I'd like to do, Jacob," Ben said as they stood to say goodnight.

"I'd like the three of us to take a nice long ride tomorrow, and see just what it is we'll have to do to meld these two properties into one. Some cold meat and hard biscuits in the saddle bags, and we'll make it a day."

No one argued, and all had smiles as they discussed particular ideas. Ben wanted to increase the sheep herds, Chance wanted to increase the horse cavvy, and Jenny reminded both that they would need hired hands, "and soon."

"I'm home," Chance said, for about the tenth time. "That was my last ride, Jennifer. I'm just so glad that all of this has happened to me. Five years ago, I would have scoffed, laughed at the thought of being a daddy, being a husband, being tied down to a ranch. Thank God I met you."

He took his wife in his arms, hugged her as tight as he dared, considering her condition and all, and started walking her toward the bedroom. "Good night, Ben," Chance said.

"Good night, Fists Like Iron," came the reply.

-end-

About the Author:

I'm a member of The Western Fictioneers, the organization for professional authors of Western novels and short stories, and a member of the International Thriller Writers.

My beautiful wife Patty and I live on a small hobby farm about twenty miles north of Reno, Nevada, sharing space with a couple of fine horses, a flock of egg-producing chickens, and some breeding rabbits. You're always welcome to visit. I need help cleaning those corrals.

Social Media Links:

Facebook: https://www.facebook.com/johnny.gunn.31

Blog: http://johnny-gunn.blogspot.com/

Twitter: https://twitter.com/johnnygunn11

If you liked this book, please check out Johnny Gunn's other books from Solstice Publishing

Jacob Chance U.S. Marshall

Land law, water rights, deeds of ownership? Boring. Unless of course, people are shooting at you because of them. The Civil War has disrupted thousands of lives, including that of Sarah Jackson, whose husband was killed for not joining the Confederate Army in Georgia. Sarah and her daughter flee to Nevada Territory and are eligible for homestead rights. After claiming her one hundred sixty acres in the lush Golden Valley, her world crumbles again.

Banker Preston Miller claims he owns the entire Golden Valley and all the water in the Good Hope River. Jackson cries foul in a letter to the U.S. Attorney in San Francisco, and Jacob Chance, U.S. Marshal rides to Preston, Nevada Territory to "settle this little land dispute."

He finds many in the town fear for their lives and livelihood, but it takes just a few shots from big guns to convince them to back the marshal. Lives are lost, buildings are burned, the town itself is in jeopardy, and the U.S. Marshal finds himself up against an army. Anarchy is the rule in the Golden Valley.

Fighting the bad guys is hard enough, he also finds himself fascinated by the daughter of one of the ranchers whose property he is trying to save. Will the town survive? Will the ranches survive? Is romance in the air? All the answers are inside these covers.

http://bookgoodies.com/a/B00XWBQ0OO

Paradise Challenged

Thornton Holiday is a murderer and a bank robber. He's a man with a plan—a plan to create an outlaw haven in the New Mexico community of Plainsville. The village is overrun with the meanest outlaws in the west and fights back with the help of a fourteen-year-old boy who demands to be considered a man.

http://bookgoodies.com/a/B015QFSMAS

So Young So Dead

The vicious murder of a young girl leads to the disintegration of the Sandesta County Sheriff's Department. A homophobic district attorney, a misogynist sergeant of detectives, and a serial killer all come together in So Young, So Dead. Many issues facing law enforcement today are as much social issues as they are criminal. They have all found a home in Sandesta County.

http://bookgoodies.com/a/B0193RHXXW

Miss Minerva's Sheriff

She was tall and thin, had a .45 strapped on, and said she wanted to make him the happiest man in the world. The sheriff had a reputation that said he was tough, fair, and could shoot straight, but could he stand up to Miss Minerva? And what will the town think? A quirky western romance, Miss Minerva's Sheriff is set in the little Nevada community of Ione, once the Nye County Seat, during the worst mid-winter blizzard ever. He saved her once, now it's her turn.

http://bookgoodies.com/a/B01CEUMZTW

www.ingramcontent.com/pod-product-compliance
Lightning Source LLC
Chambersburg PA
CBHW051135020726
47501CB00005B/1515